SHORT STORIES

— FOR THE —

DARING

YACHTSMAN

Printed in Australia
Cover and internal design by Shawline Publishing Group Pty Ltd
First Printing: June 2023

Shawline Publishing Group Pty Ltd
www.shawlinepublishing.com.au

Paperback ISBN 978-1-9229-9330-4
Ebook ISBN 978-1-9229-9335-9

Distributed by Shawline Distribution and Lightningsource Global

A catalogue record for this work is available from the National Library of Australia

More great Shawline titles can be found by scanning the QR code below.
New titles also available through Books@Home Pty Ltd.
Subscribe today at www.booksathome.com.au or scan the QR code below.

SHORT STORIES

— FOR THE —

DARING

YACHTSMAN

IB SVANE

Many people influenced our lives during the time in Mexico and the Pacific crossing. Special thanks to:

Mike and Shelly, La Paz Yachts

Robert on "Pachuca"

Keith and Susan on "C'est la Vie"

Don and Debbie on "Buena Vista"

Gary on "Dash"

Katie and Phil on "Avalon"

David and Kimberly on "Kialoa III"

Michael Latte on "Narwhale"

Ken and Linda on "Rosebud"

Neal and Ruth on "Ruthea"

Hans Erik from Copenhagen, Katie on Avalon and Heather from Port Lincoln helped me to make sense of my stories.

Carin Haldane, Port Lincoln, provided editorial help and support.

My wife Yadranka was bravely by my side, for which I am grateful.

I would like to thank Shawline Publishing and the editors for having faith in my stories. I am grateful for the tireless efforts of the production team and the careful editing by Cathy Adams. Without you all, there would not have been any book.

Prologue

The short stories in this collection may be regarded as fictional, but there is a nucleus of truth in every one of them, some more than others. In March 2011, my wife and I joined the "Pacific Puddle Jump", a sailing yacht rally from Mexico to French Polynesia, organised by the editor of the yacht magazine "Latitude 38". The editor also organises a rally from the US West Coast to Cabo San Lucas, on the tip of the California Peninsula at the mouth of the Sea of Cortez, called "The Baja Ha-Ha". Many participants in that rally join the Pacific Puddle Jump later in the season. Both events bring yachts together from all over the world.

Many of the participants have never sailed in the open seas or crossed an ocean before. It is a challenge for the first-timers. Leaving the coast of Mexico, the first landfall is likely to be the Marquesas some 24 days later. You will not likely meet anyone while crossing, but you will have radio contact with other rally participants. For many, arriving in the Marquesas is a relief and even a spiritual experience. The smell of land, flowers and earth reaches your nostrils long before you see land. The feeling of 'we made it!' can be overwhelming. From there on, it is island hopping with some week-long sailing distances.

The crossing from Mexico to the Marquesas is not without its dangers. The Equator must be crossed before 130 degrees west to reach the Marquesas. Otherwise, the trans-equatorial current will push you to the Tuamotu Archipelago, a large area with many low coral atolls you may or may not see on the radar. Weather can be miserable, with numerous squalls catching the unprepared. But sailing in the open sea changes people; they will never be the same yachtsmen or women again. You will eventually feel the open ocean is a safer place than an unknown coast.

Some people say that a boat has a soul. John Steinbeck certainly did in his book "The Log from the Sea of Cortez". I am inclined to agree with him because out there, you depend on your boat, and your boat depends on you. You can feel when your boat is happy or not. Somehow, your boat will tell you where to go.

It has been said before that the journey itself is not as important as the people you meet. That is undoubtedly true. Bad weather, hazards and misfortunes are quickly forgotten, but people are not. When onboard a yacht, you have left your worries behind. A busy schedule keeps your mind away from previous problems. Now it's all about sailing and keeping your boat happy. Warm friendships develop between ocean cruisers when they meet, and tears flow when saying goodbye. But you will meet again somewhere and reconnect as if you have not been separated. A mutual understanding of the life at sea is always there but mostly unspoken because we yachtsmen and women understand.

The first seven stories are from the coast of Mexico. The following five are from the crossing to the Marquesas and further on until the last log before arriving on the Australian East Coast. Then the attention is on what can happen to you when choosing to sail the long distance across the Indian Ocean from Cape Town to Fremantle, as so many single handers have done following the Roaring Forties.

The three last ones are from Scandinavia — my home waters earlier in life.

Finally, a poem, or rhyme, about loneliness, "The Single Hander".

I hope, dear reader, that you someday will cross an ocean. Let not these stories discourage you. Just lean back and enjoy while your boat sails itself.

Content

Acapulco

Linda and Mike had planned their Mexican trip for a long time. They had purchased a 39-foot yacht and joined the cruising course in the yacht club of Alameda. Both Mike and Linda enjoyed the classes and the friendship of the many prospective cruisers they met. Mike knew that the yacht he bought was mainly built for the charter market as a weekend sailing vessel. But he got it cheap.

Linda adored the boat with its spacious cabins, large galley with a modern gas oven and a comfortable lounge. But it was the bathroom that gave her the image of life on a yacht cruising along the Mexican coast and the sunny Sea of Cortez. In privacy, she could stand up and shower with both cold and hot water available.

'The toilet is electric — can you imagine!' she told her best friend.

Mike explained to her in technical terms that the previous owner had installed a water maker which would produce freshwater when cruising with the engine running. She was not interested. The only thing she cared about was that freshwater was available. All the technical stuff and how to sail the thing was Mike's problem — she trusted him. What eventually convinced her that the yacht was the boat for her was the stern platform, which had a ladder and a hand shower. Linda could get in and out of the water easily and rinse herself off. She boasted to her best friend as if she had to persuade her to come along. But for Linda, it was all about convincing herself — and her best friend — that the decision to take the Mexican cruising trip was hers and Mike's, and not Mike's alone.

Linda had no intention of joining the yacht captain classes. She was happy to join most of the other wives and just concentrate on a coxswain certificate. The instructors knew, of course, that a successful yachting course had to be for both spouses. The final issue of certificates had to be formal but leave everybody with a feeling of achievement. The participants did not doubt the courses were taught by professional maritime people, because they always wore smart Navy uniforms with gold stripes on their shoulder straps. For the instructors, it was all about securing satisfaction — the course fees and the number of participants were always on their mind.

The final test for the season's yachting group was a Sunday trip from Alameda to East Bay, Angel Island. Couples were organised in five sailing vessels, each with an instructor and a deckhand. The yachts were loaded with lunch provisions, including Champagne, to be consumed when the final certificates were awarded. Linda and Mike were allocated berths on the yacht "Tiburon", owned by one of the leading instructors. Before departure, the hopeful yacht students studied the day's tides, currents, and winds; it looked to be a fine day.

As they left the yacht harbour, the men admired the Tiburon and all the smart gadgets on board, while the women were chattering away discussing and admiring the recently bought foul weather gear. For them, looking smart and wearing the latest maritime fashion was important. For the men, it was all about sailing, because from now on, they were on their own. But they did not need to worry, the instructor and the deckhand had everything under control, and in sunshine and light winds, the fleet cruised leisurely towards East Bay and the lunch.

Upon arrival, anchors were dropped, and experiences loudly

communicated across the water to the wives on the other four boats. For those interested in going ashore, dinghies were launched to return when the lunch was ready. When everybody was back in their respective vessel, each yachting student was given a multiple-choice questionnaire — one for the yacht captain candidates and one for coxswain candidates. The instructor and the deckhand assisted if anybody found the questions difficult. The questionnaires were collected, and the deckhand disappeared below for assessment. Shortly after, he appeared with the marked questionnaires and a handful of signed certificates. Naturally, they all passed. The instructor congratulated all the new captains and coxswains and handed over the certificates. Then he opened his briefcase and pulled out a stack of licences in a watertight plastic envelope with a passport size photograph of each yachting student, signed by the director of The Diploma Company Yacht Training School. In relief, they all got stuck into the lunch and the Champagne. A couple of hours later, the armada of five sailing vessels zigzagged back to the Alameda Marina.

Mike and Linda joined a group of local yachties who had their sights on the annual migration to the blue waters of Mexico and the Sea of Cortez by signing up to the rally "Baja Ha-Ha" departing early November from San Diego. The group had several Sunday meetings in the yacht club to discuss their preparations and take advice from anybody who had previously made the trip. The men inspected one another's boats, discussing everything from the top of the mast through the rigging down to the bolts securing the keel to the hull. Of particular interest were the electronic navigation gear and the latest VHF radios. Nearly all invested in brand new radar equipment, and of course, automatic steering equipment; the autopilot. The talk progressed to route and weather planning and whether paper charts were needed now that all had invested in the latest model of plotters.

The ladies of the yachties enjoyed the company of newfound friends and met at cafes to discuss food and provisions which they brought to their boats by the supermarket trolley loads. They all had fridges on board and power from the dock ensured nothing was wasted. Linda asked her husband whether it was possible to install a freezer on board, but he politely declined, saying such a gadget would quickly exhaust their batteries. There was a small freezing compartment in their fridge, but Linda found the capacity far too little. Reluctantly, she carried her purchases of roasts, whole chickens, steaks, and packages of BBQ sausages back home. She swiftly rejected Mike's suggestion of buying bags of beef jerky they could store in the last available space under the bathroom sink.

'We have already decided that this space is for my toiletries!' she said with a stern, defensive look.

Mike knew that driving his argument further was a lost cause. Every Sunday, Mike nervously watched the water level creep up the sides of their 39-foot yacht, passing the waterline by two inches. His fellow yachties assured him it was not a worry. They were not heading into a storm or anything like it. They had been told many times that going south was a fair wind experience, as an extended holiday with parties planned at every anchorage.

Then Neil, the owner of Tiburon, appeared at their regular meetings. Neil was a retired Army officer who had commanded an armoured vehicle platoon in several conflicts. They all looked up to him because he was their leading instructor at the yacht training school.

'Guys,' he said while rolling the ends of his red moustache, 'I'm going to San Diego. If you want, we can cruise south together?'

There was a pause. Then Mike asked nervously, 'Are you sure?'

'Yes,' was the response. 'I'm joining the Baja Ha-Ha to Cabo. It's more fun when you have company.'

When the yacht ladies joined the meeting, Neil introduced his wife Sue to the company.

Sue took over describing what lay ahead.

'Oh,' she said, 'cruising down the California coast in the long, lazy days of late summer is a joy. Bays and harbours dot the shore well-situated for comfortable day sailing with slow-paced mornings progressing into exhilarating afternoons galloping ahead of the sea breeze to reach the next anchorage by sundown. In every location, there are attractions to amuse even the most seasoned cruiser.'

Sue paused, enjoying the gasps of excitement from the lady yachties.

'Well,' said Neil, 'are you coming with us or not?' He eyed the yachties as if he had commanded an attack.

But there were no signs of retreat; they all clapped and thanked Sue and Neil for joining them.

'We will leave early October, so we have lots of time before the Baja Ha-Ha departs in early November.'

Now the aspiring cruisers had reached the point of no return. Not going would cause them to lose face, which would likely leave them friendless.

At sunrise, they all gathered in the marina, ready to leave. During the previous evening, the last load of booze was stored onboard. All had a sleepless night. After a stressful departure, the yachts motored out of the marina in close pursuit of Tiburon, with Sue at the helm. Outside the breakwater, Neil hoisted all sails and in the light northerly breeze Tiburon sped away. The five yachts were left behind, but soon a flurry of febrile activity descended on the boats. With swearing and shouting, the mainsails were set followed by the furling genoas. They all had their autopilots and engines running, leaving the wives to be look-outs while their husbands attended the sails and sheets. There was screaming and swearing; only luck prevented major collisions. But soon, all boats settled down and followed Tiburon like a gaggle of geese.

Mike eventually got control over his yacht and was able to stop the engine. He adjusted the course on the autopilot and the sheets of the sails. Suddenly, the five yachts found themselves in a race to catch the Tiburon. Except for Tiburon, all men were at the helm with their wives sitting in the cockpit trying to find a comfortable spot avoiding saltwater spray.

At lunchtime, a brisk north-westerly picked up. Having left the pre-packed sandwiches below, Mike felt hungry after a long stressful morning and asked Linda to fetch his sandwiches. Linda looked firmly ahead and answered briskly,

'Fetch them yourself!'

Within thirty minutes, Linda was lying down with a wet towel over her head. She had vomited twice in the cockpit. Mike had tried to get the ship bucket out, but Linda refused to move, preventing him from opening the hatch. Now the stern shower came in handy, and Mike washed the vomit overboard.

With Tiburon safely tucked in behind the breakwater at Half Moon Bay, the five pursuing yachts arrived one by one, with all the wives lying flat in the cockpit with wet towels over their faces.

A quiet evening descended on the yachts, arguments and yelling subsided to the sound of sizzling BBQs accompanied by loud giggling and talking as the late five o'clock martinis reached the bottom of empty stomachs. Sue visited all five cruising yachts, declining the offered drinks and nibbles. She diplomatically suggested to the seasoned yacht captains that maybe they should allow their wives at the helm to avoid, or at least reduce, the tendency of seasickness. After a bit of partying among the yachts, the armada fell asleep on their bunks to the raucous barking and snorting from the sea lion colony on the breakwater.

The Tiburon, with the five aspiring cruising yachts in tow, proceeded southwards to San Diego stopping overnight and rounding Point Conception, the "Cape Horn of California" as a milestone on the passage down the West Coast. After experiencing the Channel Islands, they headed straight for San Diego and the protection of Shelter Island.

With great expectations, they entered La Playa Basin and eventually found their pre-booked berths in the yacht club marina. The excitement of arrival was overwhelming and hard to control. Shops with marine fashion were plentiful, and all had to be investigated. The five women made shopping their favourite pastime, and Mike soon discovered his budget had not considered the extravaganza in restaurants and cafes and the further need for additional dockside fashion. He, and the other now seasoned yacht captains, looked forward to their departure as the controlling agent for their out-of-control negative cash flow. Now there were only a few more obstacles: the Ha-Ha Welcome Party, the Annual Ha-Ha Kick-Off Costume Party and BBQ, and the Baja Ha-Ha Kick-Off Parade. It was a nervous time of preparation before departure south, a week later.

On November 1, a climax was reached. Mike ran around like a headless goose to skipper-check-in, mandatory skippers' meeting, and then to join his wife Linda at the Annual Ha-Ha Kick-Off Costume Party and BBQ outside a major marine store which sponsored the event. Linda had secured two costumes, one for herself as Dolly Parton, and one for Mike as Elvis Presley. The majority of attending crews seemed to prefer to be pirates, but that didn't bother Linda; she had been a fan of Elvis since she was a teenager. Mike had no costume preference at all; he just wanted to go back to his yacht and his bunk. Linda handed him a drink and as the party-goers absorbed a steady flow of long-drinks Mike enjoyed being Elvis.

It took time before the BBQ was ready. For many, the event was the first time they were introduced to the Mexican drink, the margarita. The tequila had an immediate effect, and the noisy crowd partied close to midnight until the first police patrol appeared.

At 10 a.m., the following morning, the America's Cup starting gun from the Sport Fishing Association of California rang through the ears of some heavy-headed cruisers, launching the Baja Ha-Ha parade. The parade proceeded to the offshore start outside San Diego Bay off Point Loma. At 11 a.m. sharp, the fleet was off. A fresh north-westerly breeze brought the fleet to Ensenada, 65 miles south. For most boats, arrival in Ensenada, the first port of entry to Mexico, was a relief, and everyone looked forward to an early night.

The following weeks, the Baja Ha-Ha fleet proceeded south in a north-westerly breeze, jumping from harbour to anchorage, from anchorage to harbour, and from party to party, with no concerns about how they would go back. Few knew that going home, the infamous up-hill bash, was a slow motoring experience which could last weeks on end unless the cruisers decided to sail back via Hawaii!

Excitement and relief mounted among the Baja Ha-Ha fleet during the last leg from Bahia Santa Maria to Cabo San Lucas, and it reached an insurmountable high when Bahia San Lucas appeared ahead; the first taste of tropical paradise after 710 nautical miles since San Diego. More than 100 cruising yachts and big game sport fishers lined moorings and anchorages of the outer harbour. Boats came and went. The dream came alive.

After mooring and check-ins, the crews joined the "Can't Believe We Cheated Death Again Dance and Party Madness for the Young Heart at Squid Roe until the Last Body Falls". Mike, Linda, and their cruiser friends were in a state of exaggerated hilarity. They partied most of the night, only to wake up to reality at the awards presentations in Marina Cabo San Lucas. Days got slower and so did the final farewell. Tears and hugs flowed as boats, one by one, were farewelled. Most sailed into the Sea of Cortez to La Paz to meet again at the La Paz Beach Party at La Costa Restaurant to join in the Mexican folk dancing. Others had heard the consistent call from their exhausted livers and proceeded north to Puerto Escondido "hidden port" to rest.

Soon, there were only two boats left. The Tiburon with Sue and Neil and the 39-foot yacht with Linda and Mike on board.

One quiet afternoon, Linda and Mike invited Sue and Neil on their boat for a coffee. They sat around the table in the cockpit and watched the boats coming and going. They all had a couple of relaxed days and left Baja Ha-Ha behind them. The conversation revolved about the up-coming sailfish fishing competition as they watched all the fast fishing boats arrive with their long fishing rods on the sides of the wheelhouse and the flying bridge.

The conversation turned to the future and what plans they had. Mike said that they probably would spend a month or so with a lazy life in the Sea of Cortez.

'What about you?' Mike asked.

'Well,' said Neil, 'we are going south to Acapulco. I have to meet a business associate, but we will just wander down the coast and enjoy all the anchorages. We will look forward to revisiting Banderas Bay, Las Hadas and Laguna de Navidad.'

'Acapulco!' cried Linda with excitement. 'Can you remember the old Elvis movie "Fun in Acapulco"? — I just loved that movie. Remember how Elvis jumped from the cliffs and the beautiful Ursula Andrews, and all the fabulous songs? Gosh, that was great. I would like to go to Acapulco — imagine if Elvis turned up!'

Neil looked at Linda with a smile and said, 'Elvis has surely died, but the Clavadistas are still jumping from the cliffs some 130 feet above the sea; it's quite spectacular. Maybe you will see the ghost of Elvis.'

Mike joined their conversation. 'I hate to disappoint you, but Elvis never went to Mexico; he was banned, and everything was shot elsewhere.'

Linda looked disappointed, but Sue came to her rescue.

'Mike, how can you be that cruel? Whether it was shot in

Acapulco or not doesn't matter; we all have the right to live our dreams.'

'Yes,' said Linda, 'I want to go to Acapulco and look for the ghost of Elvis.'

She looked firmly at her husband. Neil opened his hands in gesture and said, 'If you want to go with us, you're welcome.'

Sue nodded.

After Sue and Neil had left, the couple discussed their prospects. Mike wanted to go north, but Linda wanted to go south.

'It's a long way to Acapulco,' said Mike.

But Linda had an argument and said, 'We are not experienced sailors, although you pretend to be. We now have the chance to sail with two very experienced sailors who have cruised in Mexico for many years, so why not?'

'All right, I give in,' Mike said with a sigh.

Back on the Tiburon, Sue asked Neil, 'Do you think the 39-foot yacht would be a good courier?'

'Why not?' said Neil. 'There are several hidden spaces below which are not that easy to find. It is a result of the sandwich construction they use for this type of bucket.'

Sue nodded and said, 'That's good; we will take them along.'

The following days, Neil and Sue outlined the route they had decided to take to reach Acapulco. They would make an overnight trip to Mazatlan on the mainland and spend a couple of days there before sailing on to Isla Isabela and San Blas. Sue became excited by the thought, but Mike and Linda worried about the overnight trip — they had never sailed at night before. But Sue said, 'Don't you worry, it will be fine. You can't imagine how beautiful Isla Isabela is. The island is full of nesting frigate birds and blue-footed boobies; there is a bird research station there.'

She looked at Linda, who got excited when she heard what Sue said. Sue added, 'There are fishermen on the island, we might get a bucketload of lobsters, if not, then we will get them in San Blas. They are so nice on the barbie.'

After a couple of days in Cabo, where the girls shopped in the supermarket and browsed all the shops available, the two cruisers left for Mazatlan. The day was calm, and they motored along, setting sails with every puff of air. The fair weather continued during the night. After an evening meal, Mike rested on his bunk next to the navigation table while the motor was running and the auto-pilot was steering. The navigation lights were on. Linda sat comfortably on the cushions in the cockpit, reading a book under the small lamp Mike had installed. Occasionally, she looked at the radar where Mike had set the alarm to 2 nautical miles. Linda could see a blinking dot three miles ahead of them, which Mike had explained was the Tiburon. There was nothing else. Before midnight, Linda woke Mike as she slipped into bed while complaining about the noisy engine. Mike made himself a cup of coffee and took over Linda's cushions, stretching his legs on the cockpit bench, enjoying the sailing and the spectacular starry sky. During the night, he nodded on and off, but everything went well.

In the early morning, he spotted the coastline with the rising sun. They quickly found the narrow entrance to the marina and moored next to the Tiburon with Sue and Neil, who greeted them with a morning glass of Champagne. Several other cruisers joined in.

Sailing down the coast was mainly day cruises in light winds and motoring. They anchored every afternoon and Linda thought they were magical places, but Isla Isabela was her favourite. She wanted to stay on, but they needed provisions. The lobsters appeared in San Blas as Sue had promised and they enjoyed the small town and market. From there they reached the spectacular Banderas Bay, where large cruise ships came and went from the dock of Puerto Vallarta.

'It is too busy there. I suggest we go to La Cruz on the other side. It is a cozy place,' Neil said, and so they did.

Sue took Linda to a jewellery shop and showed her the Mexican fire opals. She was stunned by their beauty. Back on the boat, she persuaded Mike to buy some for her.

'It's soon our anniversary, remember!' Linda exclaimed.

Mike obeyed when Sue told him the price. He knew nothing about fire opals but trusted her judgement. Linda was thrilled and showed the opals to her husband and Neil — she was happy.

The cruising south became even more magical as they visited Las Hadas and further on Laguna de Navidad. Linda and Sue spent two days in the hotel swimming pool while Mike and Neil were reading. Mike found it difficult to relax because he expected a large hotel bill. The two cruising yachts eventually reached a small, sheltered harbour. In Mike's pilot, it was Puerto Escondido, while in Neil's it was Papanoa. A visit to town cleared up the confusion; both names were on signs along the road. Neil explained that there are many small harbours in Mexico which were called Puerto Escondido, but he asked one of the locals, and they called the harbour Papanoa — the port for Noah's Ark.

When they met on Tiburon for their usual five o'clock drinks, Neil said, 'I'm sorry, but we must leave very early. I have this meeting with a business associate. I would like to get it out of the way. I had an email from him, and he will come from Mexico City. You shouldn't have any problem sailing to Acapulco, which is just around the corner, so to speak.'

Mike and Linda sat quietly, holding on to their drinks. Sue looked at the couple and said, 'Don't look that worried. It's just down the coast a bit from here. When you are in the bay, keep left, and you will see the anchorage outside several marinas and a large terminal. It's easy!'

Mike toughened himself up and said, 'We are not worried, it will be fine. We will take our time. We will stay here another day before going to Acapulco. That will give you time to finish your business.'

They had another drink and said goodbye.

In their yacht, Mike and Linda left Papanoa at nine in the morning after a full day relaxing on the anchorage. The sea was flat calm. Under a blue sky and shining sun, they motored out of the harbour with Mike at the helm. Linda was in her usual position on pillows on the cockpit bench reading an old fashion magazine she picked up in the yacht club in Cabo San Lucas. Now and then she looked over the flat, calm sea.

After hours of sailing, Mike said with an excited voice, 'I think we have a couple of whales ahead.'

Linda jumped up. 'Give me the binoculars,' she said.

Mike handed her the glass and Linda looked ahead with excitement.

'Wow,' she said, 'isn't that fantastic? Can't you sail any closer?'

'I don't want to go too close, but I will try. They may just dive and disappear,' Mike said.

The whales did not move much and as they came closer, Linda, still excited, exclaimed, 'I think it's two whales and a little calf.'

John lowered the speed as they slowly sailed towards the whales, now only about 100 feet away.

Then, with a massive "bang" the stern of their yacht was lifted up. With a grinding sound, the engine stopped. The wheel was shaking and got stuck. As Mike looked over the side, he saw a giant whale tail smacking violently into the side of his yacht, turning the boat. He looked up in disbelief and saw Linda in complete shock.

At that moment, the boom with a sagging mainsail came swinging over the cockpit and hit Mike's bald head with a hollow sound. Mike fell backwards, and unconscious slid out through the opening to the after platform and into the water. The last Linda saw of her husband was his naked feet sticking up in the air as his body disappeared.

Linda was at first mute but then screamed and screamed her lungs out.

'Mike, Mike,' she screamed, 'come back!'

But Mike was way below.

Linda sat down wholly paralysed as the boat slowly drifted westward. She had little voice left. As Linda looked out, she saw a motor vessel in the distance. She shouted while jumping up and down, waving her arms. The motor vessel didn't notice and continued its course. She looked down and saw a stream of water coming out of a hole in the hull. She heard the low noise of an electric motor running.

Linda calmed herself and started to think. *What to do, what to do?*

She grabbed the microphone of the VHF radio, pressed the button, and shouted, 'Help, help!'

She suddenly remembered something from her coxswain course and shouted in the microphone, 'Mayday, Mayday, Mayday'.

She looked at the radio and realised it had no power; she could not see the selected channel. She smashed the microphone into the cover and cried, 'Bloody shit, bloody shit!'

Now what? she thought.

She remembered something about flares — the coloured sticks in a plastic bag. She had no idea how to use them, but looked around to see as if they were on display in the cockpit. Linda went below and looked everywhere but found none. She lifted every cushion and searched every corner of the boat but found none. Linda sat down on the soft bench while tears and mascara flowed down her cheeks. She dried them away with her hands, grabbed a towel and cried more. The boat drifted further and further offshore.

Linda got up in the cockpit and looked over the calm ocean; there was not a boat in sight. She sat down and looked at the setting sun. The sounds of flowing water and the electric motor were gone. She needed a drink and went below. Her feet got wet, and she looked around. Plywood floorboards were floating. Linda sat down, pulled her feet up, supporting herself with pillows.

Wait till I get hold of you, Mike — this time it will be a divorce, she thought while biting a broken nail.

She poured herself a large tequila, had a sip and leaned back. It was getting dark. Linda had a few more tequilas and dozed a bit. Drunk, she forced herself through the water in the cabin and up on the deck and screamed,

'I will get you, Mike!'

She could not stand up, grabbed the rail, and pulled herself down into the cabin to the soft cushions, which were now wet. Linda laid down after another couple of tequilas.

Two hours later, a 39-foot yacht reached the muddy bottom of the sea. There was one passenger on board. Before long, Linda had caught up with her husband, who introduced her to the Ghost of Elvis.

Early afternoon, the Tiburon, with Sue and Neil onboard anchored in Bahia Acapulco at Terminal Maritima off the two marinas. They motored their dinghy to a small beach and dragged it a bit up on the sand. After locking the dinghy to the dock, the couple walked up the steep cobblestoned Teniente José Azueta to La Quebrada. Neil could feel the weight of his money belt and the handgun he carried in a shoulder holster under his left arm.

After the long walk along La Quebrada, they arrived at a small plaza with the entry to the Clavadistas de La Quebrada. A group of tourists were waiting for diving performances to begin. Sue and Neil sat down at a shaded table outside Hotel Mirador and ordered two marguerites. They waited. The sun was just above the horizon, and Neil's business associate had not arrived. Neil looked at Sue and gave a deep sigh. She looked back, worried, and said, 'I think we should go back before it is getting dark. You can call him tomorrow.'

The couple got up, and Neil paid their bill. They walked back down the cobblestoned La Quebrada.

In the early morning, just after sunrise, a fast police vessel carrying a Mexican flag came alongside the Tiburon. It had a dinghy with a small outboard in tow. A sailor jumped onboard while another jumped in the dinghy and took off the outboard. The sailors secured the outboard at its place on the cockpit rail. They dragged the dinghy up on the deck and prepared to tow the yacht. There were no other people on board. The police knew that. They had recovered two headless bodies lying in the gutter of Teniente José Azueta.

Boat Envy

Kraken

There are certain varieties of whales in the seas of Iceland that may be eaten by men. One of these is called humpback; this fish is large and very dangerous to ships. It has a habit of striking at the vessel with its fins and of lying and floating just in front of the prow where sailors travel. Though the ship turns aside, the whale will continue to keep in front, so there is no choice but to sail upon it—but if a ship does sail upon it, the whale will throw the vessel and destroy all on board.

From *"The King's Mirror"*. Composed in Old Norse during King Hákon Hákonarson's reign (1217–1263).

Comfortable in the cockpit on board a 42-foot sailing yacht, Sunset Folly, Tom, and Laureen were sailing south along the Mexican coast. In light winds, they had left Mazatlan for the Island of Isla Isabel, off the small town of San Blas, both popular anchorages for yachts cruising along the coast. It was an overnight passage, but they were not alone. They were in the company of a smaller, green 33-foot sloop. Tom and Laureen came from San Diego with the Baja Ha-Ha, a two-week cruisers rally from San Diego to Cabo San Lucas on the southern tip of the Californian Peninsula and the entrance to the Sea of Cortez.

Every autumn, the rally brought sailors to Mexico with dreams of endless sunshine and safe ocean cruising. Many were joining the cohort of "grey nomads" who spent the American winter in the sunny Sea of Cortez, putting their boats on the hard, escaping north in their campers as the hurricane season approached in April and the spring north of the border was in full bloom. Most have only had yachts for a short time but joined navigation courses in the local yacht club — an exciting approach to an enjoyable retirement.

Most yachts would not stay in Cabo San Lucas but proceed up in the Sea of Cortez and stay in the marinas or anchorages of La Paz, a small town not as busy as Cabo and less popular with the game fishers and expensive motor yachts.

What attracted cruisers to La Paz was the charm of the little Mexican town, but also Club Cruceros, the cruisers' club.

Among the many grey nomads were another group of yachties, who lived a reticent life away from restaurants and cafés. They were retired service people, many recovering from being badly wounded, living on a meagre pension provided by the US military. When needed, the retired service people would make an annual trip by bus to the military hospital in San Diego, where they receive free medical aid.

Tom and Laureen met Andy and Sue at the coffee hour at Club Cruceros. Andy was sitting on a bench while Sue was talking to a group of women, including Laureen. Tom spotted him, sat down next, told him it was their first time in La Paz, and looked forward to the coming cruising season. Andy, who was in his early sixties, did not say much but nodded and smiled at Tom's description of the many problems they had encountered since they left San Diego.

After a while, the other women left, leaving Laureen alone with Sue. She liked her company despite the age difference. Laureen asked, 'Why don't you and your husband come over to our boat for dinner tonight?'

There was a pause. Then Sue quietly said, 'I'm afraid I have to say no. You see, I am suffering from "boat envy"; I can't be on other boats.'

'Boat envy,' Laureen said, 'What is that?'

There was another pause. Sue took Laureen aside, putting her arm under hers and walked away from the clubhouse.

'This is embarrassing for me,' Sue said, 'But we only have a small boat. We have all our belongings there, and if I visit other boats, I get so depressed that I can't handle it. Andy is often in terrible pain, so much that I can't stay on board. Instead, I walk the dock and even the streets in the middle of the night before I can return. It takes a while before his medicine works.'

Laureen was shocked and did not know what to say. The two women stopped at the bench where Andy and Tom were sitting. Tom said, 'We better go back to our boat. It's already lunchtime.'

The two men got up, and Tom noticed that Andy's left leg made a strange noise but did not say anything.

Andy and Sue's boat was not far from the berth where Tom and Laureen's yacht was moored. Laureen watched Andy and Sue as they helped one another into their cockpit.

'Tom, I think Andy has real medical problems. Sue told me he has the Purple Heart and many decorations from his army time. He retired wounded.'

'Yes,' Tom said, 'I noticed he has a problem walking. I think he has an artificial leg.'

Tom and Laureen ate their lunch in silence, both thinking about the meeting at Club Cruceros.

'You know,' Laureen said, 'I invited them for dinner, but Sue declined. She said she suffered from "boat envy". I will not let her get away with that. I will make up a couple of plates of finger food, and at five, we will go over to their boat with a bottle of wine.'

Tom and Laureen walked over to Andy and Sue's boat at five sharp, the cocktail time. Tom was balancing a large tray with food. Laureen pulled the shroud and said loudly, 'Knock, knock.'

Andy's head popped out of the cabin, looked at Tom and Laureen, and then at the bottle of wine Laureen carried. With a big smile, Laureen said, 'Please, join us for a glass of wine.'

Both Andy and Sue manoeuvered themselves out of the narrow cabin entrance and into the cockpit. Most spaces were taken by plastic boxes full of stuff, the same you'd find in people's garages stacked up along a wall.

They sat down and looked up at the dock.

'Sit down on the blanket, Tom, and stick your feet over the edge,' Laureen commanded, and Tom obeyed.

They both sat on the dock and talked to Andy and Sue sitting lower down in their cockpit. Andy looked overly grateful when Laureen handed him a large glass of wine, but his wife Sue did not. They all enjoyed the finger food, and it did not take long before Laureen ordered Tom back to their boat for another bottle. Sue said nothing.

Before long, the talk turned towards their plans for the season.

'It is still early in the cruising season, and rather than sailing in the Sea of Cortez, we have decided to go a bit south to explore the Mexican coast and the exciting natural harbours we read about in the Mexican Pilot for Yachties,' Tom explained.

'What are your plans?' Laureen asked.

Reluctantly, Sue explained, 'We are heading to San Blas. Andy's brother lives there. He has a small house. We will leave the boat there and together, travel back to San Diego in his brother's camper. Both he and Andy have medical appointments.'

'Maybe we can travel together,' Laureen said. 'We are heading to Mazatlan. Spend a night there and then to Isla Isabel for another night and then to San Blas. The trips are overnight sailing, and it is good to have company, don't you think?'

Sue agreed, and Andy nodded and said, 'Well, that's the trip we had decided on, but Leafy is not fast.'

'No problem,' Tom said, 'we are not in a hurry, and there is not much wind in the weather forecast.'

As the wine let the tongues loose, much to Laureen's dissatisfaction, Tom asked Andy why he was going for a medical.

'I have shrapnel in my back, and one is too close to my spinal cord. If I don't get it out, I will end up in a wheelchair. My brother is going for a check-up.'

Tom had half slept in the cockpit since midnight after he took over from Laureen. He started the motor then because it was flat calm. He checked on the radio with Andy and Sue on Leafy, and they motored on as well. Tom dozed on and off during the night, comfortable on a canvas-covered mattress with a couple of pillows. He woke up by the light of the rising sun, and a mug of fresh coffee poked under his nose. He looked up and saw Leafy half a mile behind his wake.

Laureen was not in her best mood, unable to sleep continuously, disturbed by the noisy engine below. In the morning sun, she joined Tom on the opposite side of the cockpit after retrieving what she considered her pillows.

'What were you doing on the deck during the night?' Laureen asked.

'Oh,' Tom answered, 'I had to fight off a shag who thought that our bow was his resting place. He was crapping all over the deck, and he wouldn't move even when I put the torch on him. I had to use the boatman's hook before he left, but as soon as I was back in the cockpit, he returned. The worst was a bloody frigate bird who decided to roost on our mast top. He crapped all over our sail.'

Tom looked proudly at Laureen as if he had rescued her from

sea monsters who were likely to devour her if he had not been handy with the boatman's hook.

'What's all the black stuff on the main? It looks like you have been marching all over it with your dirty feet.' Laureen asked with a prodding look, as if Tom was a schoolboy.

Tom looked at his feet and said, 'Yeah, when I was torching the shag, it suddenly rained, with small squids spitting ink all over the place. Don't worry; I will clean it up.'

Laureen leaned back with a deep sigh, knowing too well that Tom's cleaning intentions would never become a reality. He would, though, remove the squid carcasses when they became smelly.

After their breakfast, the wind picked up a bit, so they did not need to have the engine running. Before midday, Sunset Folly arrived on the eastern side of Isla Isabel at two spectacular contorted rock formations stretching high up. Laureen thought they looked like oversized futuristic sculptures out of place, dusted white by centuries of bird droppings. Before long, their companions arrived and anchored at a safe distance. The swell broke over rocks a bit to the north, but that didn't bother Tom and Laureen.

In the early afternoon, Laureen and Tom checked with Sue and Andy on Leafy before motoring ashore in their inflatable dinghy to explore the island. Laureen and Tom were excited to make landfall on an island so far away from the Mexican coast. They had never done that before.

On land Laureen loudly exclaimed, knowing her husband had a hearing aid. 'I can't wait to get up close and personal with the frigate birds and the blue-footed boobies with their nests and babies. I always thought I'd have to go to the Galapagos Islands to do this.'

They landed their dinghy in a tiny cove full of seasonal fishing sheds, only accessible by panga or dinghy. There was nobody there.

The couple followed a narrow but well-trodden path up in the hills. It was a bit of a hike. At the top, the noisy squeaking of hundreds of nesting birds was deafening. On the top of low trees, frigate bird nests were everywhere and on the ground were nests of blue-footed boobies. They walked carefully along the path, not disturbing the birds. The frigate birds were in full breeding plumage with their lavish red chests puffed up, much to Laureen's admiration. They agreed that their wide-eyed, fluff ball babies were ugly but, in some way, adorable. Tom thought they were wasting time but fell short of complaining when he could see Sunset Folly on anchor facing the rocks. Laureen sat down next to a couple of nests, staring at the chicks, who seemed to stare back. Tom commented rudely that he thought she looked like a roosting chook and that he was expecting a cackle when she had laid an egg. Despite angry looks from Laureen, he produced a well-sounding 'buck-buck-buck-badaaack' gaggle. Laureen got up and stared straight at Tom. She raised her clenched fist against Tom's nose and said, 'That's enough, Tom; a nose punch can be very painful!'

Tom immediately stepped backwards, lost his balance, and fell into dense vegetation covered with guano. Out of the bush came a four feet long iguana darting towards Laureen. In fright, she ran halfway down the path to the cove below, but soon returned.

'You are awful,' Laureen swore.

Covered in guano, Tom got up, receiving 'the look' he knew so well.

Tom sat on a rock and scanned the sea with his binoculars, leaving Laureen to explore the nests she wanted. After a while, he spotted Leafy leaving the anchorage, heading towards a pod of Humpback whales frolicking further towards the Mexican coast.

Tom watched Leafy getting closer to the whale pod and saw the boat stopped. He saw Sue standing up in the cockpit with her camera. Tom looked at Laureen, who was busy watching chicks. Tom said, 'Leafy is out visiting the whale pod. I can see Sue taking photos.'

Tom focused his binoculars because he saw something in the water behind the stern. Suddenly, a whale breached out of the water, swirled around next to the boat. A large flipper hit the rig, which went overboard halfway. In shock, Tom looked over his binocular to see Leafy's stern lifted out of the water on the back of the whale. Tom rushed up and, in desperation, cried, 'Laureen, Sue and Andy have been hit by a whale. The rig is overboard. We must get out there.'

Without looking at Laureen, Tom ran down the path to the cove, dragged the dinghy off the sand and jumped in. Laureen followed him. They motored out to Sunset Folly and quickly got underway, with Laureen at the helm.

Less than ten minutes later, they arrived and slowly motored alongside the damaged Leafy. Half the rigging and a broken mast were overboard, the engine was not running, and there was a foot of water in the cockpit. Andy and Sue were sitting on the cockpit bench. Sue was stone-faced and white, with Andy's arms around her. They said nothing. Tom shouted, 'Come on, get off, get over here.'

But there was no response. Tom quickly got his mask and flippers on, jumped into the water, and dragged their dinghy across. He grabbed the rail and shouted, 'Andy, get in the dinghy; I will help Sue.'

Andy turned around, looked at Tom, shook his head and said calmly, 'No need Tom, we will be all right.'

Sue appeared unresponsive. The water had reached the level of the bench. He heard a hissing sound of air escaping. In the cabin, everything was below the water. Suddenly, Tom was thrown back into the water. He quickly came up, and the Leafy was upside down. The keel was gone, leaving only a couple of damaged bolts, half the rudder too, the propeller shaft bent, and from a large hole at the stern tube, air was hissing out.

Tom dived under the boat and grabbed hold of Andy, trying to pull him up, but he could not. He tried to pull Sue out, but he could not. Back on the surface, he gasped for air and saw Leafy disappear into the deep.

Tom swam over to Laureen on Sunset Folly. He crawled up on the stern platform and secured the dinghy. Laureen was staring at Tom, who was shaking, and his face was white. He sat down on the cockpit bench. Laureen rushed below, grabbed a blanket and a bottle of water. She covered her husband with the blanket and pushed him back so he could lie down. Slowly his shakings diminished, and he accepted a drink of water. Laurene asked Tom in a solemn voice, 'Why would they not come over?'

Tom looked at Laureen with glazed eyes and answered, 'They both had their lower legs tied up to the column of the cockpit table.'

In San Blas, there was a coroner's enquiry. The US consul was present. The Mexican coroner found Laureen and Tom as credible witnesses, and in conclusion, he said, 'There but for the grace of God, go we. Every ocean sailor knows that neither they nor their boats can withstand the full fury of nature.'

Puerto Escondido my Love

(The Night of the Iguana)

At ten in the morning, Norm was waiting at the dock of the small Marina Fonatur in the muddy estuary of the Mexican town of San Blas. He was familiar with the marina and the anchorage further out. Several yachts were on anchor in Lagoon El Pozo, and a few moored in the small marina. Across the lagoon, Norm was watching a racoon searching for food. A couple of herons left their fishing places with annoying shrieks as the racoon moved along, cleaning, loitering, and scavenging along the water's edge.

Norm was impatient. The people on the yachts at anchor had agreed to meet him on the dock at ten. Those few who were in the small marina were already waiting.

At eight sharp every morning, Norm made a roll call on his VHF radio on Channel 22. He had taken that initiative for a long time, annoying many of the yachties because it was usually the yachties themselves who do that to make everybody feel like a group and share information. But Norm was once a yachtsman, or aspired to be one, and like many others, he was attracted to the coast of Mexico, where it was possible to live cheaply on a boat.

Norm had been a soldier and suffered when returning from the Vietnam War. He had been wounded twice. The transition to civilian life was difficult, and his injuries had prevented him from keeping a full-time job. His mental scars were worse than the physical ones, and the divorce came quickly. He was alone and jobless.

He bought an old sailing boat in Alameda and sailed it single-handed to La Paz on the Californian Peninsula. He never made it to his desired destination, the Sea of Cortez. Drunk, he sailed the boat onto a rock. His damaged boat ended up in one of the many 'boatyards of broken dreams' which litter the coasts of the Sea of Cortez. He thought he could do the repairs, but money was short, and the drink was easy. Things just didn't match.

Norm decided to visit a friend and took the ferry to Mazatlan. There he jumped on a bus to San Blas, a small seaside town further south. He shared the accommodation with his friend, but eventually, the drinking became too much, and his friend left him. Norm could barely survive on his meagre military pension.

Norm was not noticeable among the many poor who slept in the streets. But a local American lady, a widower, who ran a small tourist hotel did. Her name was Maxine.

Slowly, Maxine got Norm on his feet, and his drinking diminished, but not entirely. Maxine made him a guide for the guests of her hotel.

For Norm, learning was easy, but to stay sober was not. Maxine kept an eye on him. She was brought up in a strict Christian Presbyterian faith. Maxine and Norm sat with two non-alcoholic drinks on the hotel veranda every afternoon at five, the standard cocktail time for many Americans. Maxine taught him the history of San Blas, the Cerro de San Basilio, and the ruins of the church dedicated to "Our Lady of the Sailor's Rosary". She always began with a prayer to Saint Junípero Serra, a Franciscan monk and priest who sailed in 1768 from San Blas to California to set up missions and christen the native Indians.

After the prayer, which Norm accepted without enthusiasm, Maxine repeated the chronological order of the ruins.

'Remember, the Cerro de San Basilio was built as a Spanish fort in 1777 and the church, Our Lady of the Rosary, in 1769. Please repeat the years.'

Norm repeated as a little schoolboy while sipping his drink. He had already helped himself to a couple of sips of a bottle of Grand Marnier, Maxine kept in the kitchen.

Suddenly, Maxine got up and grabbed a can of mosquito spray and vigorously sprayed her arms and legs.

'Now it is "no-see-ums" time,' she said and handed the can to Norm, who followed the example.

He knew too well that the mosquitoes and sandflies in the estuary were merciless at dusk and dawn.

Satisfied, she continued, 'The most important thing to remember is the Bells of San Blas.'

It was her favourite theme every afternoon.

Maxine proudly declared, 'The Bells of San Blas must be mentioned with the deepest respect because it brings your listeners into a mood of passion, remembrance, and respect for the past. Let me recite the first stanzas alone, and then we both do it together.'

Maxine leaned back in the soft bamboo armchair, took a sip of her drink, and began.

'What say the Bells of San Blas

To the ships that southward pass

From the harbour of Mazatlan?

To them it is nothing more

Than the sound of surf on the shore,—

Nothing more to master or man.

But to me, a dreamer of dreams,
To whom what is and what seems
Are often one and the same,—
The Bells of San Blas to me
Have a strange, wild melody,
And are something more than a name.

For bells are the voice of the church;
They have tones that touch and search
The hearts of young and old;
One sound to all, yet each
Lends a meaning to their speech,
And the meaning is manifold.

They are a voice of the Past,
Of an age that is fading fast,
Of a power austere and grand;
When the flag of Spain unfurled
Its folds o'er this western world,
And the Priest was lord of the land.'

There was an extended moment of silence. Norm had listened respectfully, and Maxine's voice and compassion mesmerised him. He thought of his Catholic upbringing and the distaste he had of the church. It was not the church as such, but his father's interpretation and misuse to correct his son at any opportunity. His father would never appreciate his efforts but took delight in his failures. At eighteen, Norm signed on to the marines and left his parental home with relief.

The poem somehow gave Norm a sense of solitude, and he accepted Maxine's role and attempt to bring him back on his feet. Norm was grateful. He repeated the poem slowly and stumbling, carefully listening to Maxine's advice and corrections when he got it wrong or forgot something. Norm felt her encouragement with inner content, making him willing to learn and remember.

After the final words, Maxine looked straight at him and said, 'Do not forget to credit the poet, Henry Wadsworth Longfellow, who wrote the poem in 1882. When you can memorise these verses, I will continue with the remaining stanzas.'

Norm got to like the afternoons, because it occupied his mind. It was at night his demons came out of the woodwork. He tried to keep them away by reciting the poem and found himself sitting up in his bed with his legs over the edge, rocking back and forth, with tears running down his cheeks. The demons were there and slipped into his brain when he closed his eyes. He screamed.

At some point, Maxine got the local priest involved. He was Catholic, but that did not bother Maxine too much. After all, finding a Protestant priest in Mexico was not for a sane person. Norm was like a zombie and followed those who gave him a hand. He realised he was lucky and would do anything to keep his demons at bay.

As his mental health improved Norm spent time in the church, where he saw *the bells of San Blas*. They were taken from the old church ruins and brought to the towers of a church in the city plaza. He found a certain solitude in his former faith.

Once a week, every Friday, Maxine escorted Norm to the San Blas Social Club, one of the few watering holes in the historical port, allowing him to drink a few beers. His favourite was Corona, but he could do with Pacifico; but he could do with anything after the two. Maxine enjoyed a margarita.

Maxine had allowed him to occupy a simple room in a separate small building in the back. There was a bed, chair, and table.

Norm liked the spartan accommodation because the white walls reflected the light from a streetlamp at night. He gave a name to all the shadows so he could distinguish them from the demons.

As time passed, Norm got more roles than being a guide for the few hotel guests. He was also the handyman, which naturally pleased Maxine. Norm thought that was probably what she always had in mind.

Their relationship had been friendly, like two friends, or rather like a teacher and a schoolboy, but as Norm controlled his alcoholism, Maxine got closer. Just a little step at a time. Norm did not know whether he should respond. He had lived in celibacy for several years, and she was older than him. Norm found her attractive but had not given much thought to their relationship. He had just grabbed her hand in gratitude. He now realised that he had to give something back. Maxine expected love, at least some love. Norm was wary of what would come next, fearful that he again would grab the bottle rather than the hand. He decided to be respectful but passive.

To Norm's surprise, the priest told him straight to his face what was expected of him. He did not mention marriage, but Norm suspected that. The priest spoke to him softly about love and hinted at Maxine. He also indicated that maybe he had lovers elsewhere, which Norm denied. Returning to the hotel, Maxine was kind. At the five o'clock martini time, they sat opposite one another with their non-alcoholic drink. She directed the conversation to the Franciscan monk, Junípero Serra.

'Do you know,' she said, 'that in 1779, Franciscan missionaries under Serra's direction planted California's first sustained vineyard at Mission San Diego de Alcalá? He is the Father of California wine.'

Norm knew about Californian wine but had not paid attention to its origin. He followed the drinking habits of John Steinbeck's friends from Cannery Row. Then Maxine smilingly said, 'I have a surprise for you. Tonight, I have asked the cook to prepare a special meal for us, and with it, I have taken out a bottle of the best Californian wine we have in the house. I thought we should celebrate your recovery.'

Norm thought about the wine. Would he be able to drink wine, being on a strict ration of beer? Maxine got up from her chair and said, 'I must prepare the dinner for our guests. Do you mind giving the staff a hand and set up our table in the private section of the veranda to your liking?'

Maxine left for the kitchen, not waiting for an answer. That night, Norm and Maxine became lovers.

The last of the yachties arrived and tied their dinghies to the dock. Norm checked his list. Rick and Tanya from Third Day, George, and Mary from Pacha II, Lis and Beth from Amber Moon, Jack and Gill from Tank of Tiburon, and finally John and Gladys from Gosling.

Norm guided the group to the Plaza Principal, a short walk from the dock. There was a lot to see, and most were attracted to the many market stalls lining the plaza. Patiently, Norm brought the group to the church, Iglesia Antigua, with the famous Bells of San Blas. After a visit to a small museum, the group settled at a café for a cold drink. Norm had parked the hotel van across, and most were relieved when they realised that they didn't have to walk to the fort.

After getting everybody into the van, Norm drove along the Sinaloa Road until he reached a sign to the right saying "Del Panteon". He stopped the van outside the Church of Our Lady of the Rosary, and the group walked in.

It was in front of the church ruins that Norm showed his talent by reciting the first four stanzas of *The Bells of San Blas*. He could see his audience was impressed. When he recited the last line, 'And the Priest was lord of the land', he thought about Maxine and the priest in the church of San Blas next to the old church

Antigua across from the plaza. He felt trapped in the relationship with Maxine. But there had been no mention of marriage, and Maxine was happy when he performed in bed. Norm thought he lived in a sort of vacuum. He followed Maxine's instructions about what he could or could not drink, as he did the many months up to the time when they became lovers. He knew she took good care of him, and he was happy doing the tours and the small handyman jobs she gave him.

But something happened at the church ruin. He felt that Lis from Amber Moon showed an interest in him. She was always by his side, and the smiles she gave him were unmistakably personal. They made him shy. Jack from Tank of Tiburon whispered close to his ear in his strict military style, 'Watch out for this lady. I think she has the hots for you!'

It was as if he was warning him of an approaching enemy tank.

The next stop was the fort San Basilio, or like Norm declared in his best Spanish, 'Ruinas del Puerto de San Basilio'. With a sweeping arm, he guided the group into the fort. They all enjoyed the spectacular views over the city, the river, the sea, and the lagoon. Then they were off to lunch on the beach.

Norm had an arrangement with a beach restaurant called Playa Bonita. He got paid a small fee for bringing tourists. He always needed money. He was thinking about selling his Rolex Navigator watch because he did not need it anymore.

The lunch was a spectacular delicious dish with a mix of tropical fruits and seafood served in a hollowed-out pineapple. There was plenty of white wine and tequila, but Norm stuck to his Corona. Somehow, he felt that white wine and sex went together. But Lis sat firmly by his side and placed her hand on his hand several times. As with Maxine, he was in a vacuum and let what happened to him flow along.

The group got more and more talkative as the wine went down, and laughter easily followed. Norm found a moment to mention he had a Rolex Navigator watch for sale for $500. Jack immediately declared that he had the watch and showed his wrist. He listed all the tank battles he and his wristwatch had participated in and put effort into speaking for Norm, suggesting that the $500 offer was a bargain.

Lis placed her hand on his and whispered in his ear, 'I would like to buy your watch.'

Norm nodded, and with a quiet, 'Good.' He laid his free hand on top. A light squeeze confirmed the deal.

Lis got up from her chair and announced, 'Today is the last day with Beth onboard Amber Moon. She joined me as a crew in San Diego. We did the Baja Ha-Ha, and now the time has come for her to return to the US. We have our final dinner, and I hope you all will join us tonight, here at Playa Bonita.'

With difficulty, Norm got his group into the van and drove to the dock. They all took their dinghies back to the boats for a well-earned afternoon nap. Lis stayed with Norm while Beth fetched her backpack from Amber Moon. She held Norm's hand while they watched the dinghy with Beth sail to Amber Moon and back. Norm drove to the bus terminal, where they waved goodbye to Beth.

Back in the van, Lis did not waste her time. In a few seconds, she had released the buttons on Norm's shirt and had her hands on his hairy chest. She caressed him, pressing her nails into his naked back, they kissed. In an excited voice, Lis said, 'Drive to Hotel Pacifico. I have booked a room.'

Norm obeyed and drove to the hotel.

When Norm arrived back at Maxine's hotel, she was waiting. The question came quickly, 'Where have you been?'

Norm was still in his vacuum and did not show any feelings or anger against Maxine. He just said, 'I had to wait to drive one of my customers and her friend to the bus terminal. We missed the first bus, and then I had to drive her friend back to the dock.

She has offered me $500 for my Rolex Navigator.'

Maxine looked at Norm in a way he had never experienced before. But Norm, in his vacuum, hung the keys to the van on its hook in the reception. Maxine was not finished and sternly said, 'Father José told me that he had seen the van parked at Hotel Pacifico.'

Norm came momentarily out of his vacuum, looked straight at Maxine, and said, 'Are you telling me you have Father José spying on me?'

Maxine did not answer but looked angry. Now back in his vacuum, Norm continued, 'I had to go for a pee and number twos. You know the public toilets are dirty.'

Maxine turned around and walked into the kitchen. Norm followed slowly, and through the door opening, said, 'I am going to the Playa for dinner tonight. You can come along if you want.'

At nine, Maxine and Norm drove to Playa Bonita. Lis had organised a large table, and all the cruisers from the morning guided tour were already seated. Several new faces had arrived during the afternoon. The mood and expectations were high. With wine, tequila, and margaritas on the table and in glasses, everybody laughed and talked about their experiences sailing from La Paz to Isla Isabela and San Blas.

Norm sat with Lis on his left side and a quiet Maxine on his right. Norm had bought a bottle of wine and poured himself a glass, saying, 'Tonight I drink, you drive!'

Maxine nodded.

Norm took his Rolex out of his pocket and handed it to Lis, who gave him the money. She smiled at Norm and pinched his earlobe. Maxine was not impressed and immediately said straight to her, 'Leave my man alone, please.'

Lis smiled and said, 'Oh, jealousy, jealousy, that jealousy can eat you inside out.'

Maxine said nothing. She had made her stand.

Food arrived, and several Mexican bands tried to persuade anyone at the table to pay. First, they played and sang for a minute and then demanded money to continue.

A small boy was hanging around the table. He had a tethered iguana begging for money to allow the iguana to dance. Most at the table ignored the bands and the little boy, but another band arrived a bit later. The singer had an unusually soft voice which silenced the conversation at the table. When the singer paused, John from Gosling turned towards him, gave a Spanish request, and handed him a ten-dollar note. John smiled at Norm, raised his glass of white wine, and said, 'This one is for you, Norm, cheers!'

Everybody raised their glass and shouted, 'Cheers!"

Norm felt embarrassed. The music started in a seducing samba style, making him want to dance. The singer sang the first verse in Spanish but then continued in English.

'Esa mujer me está matando.

Me ha espinado el corazón.

Por más que trato de olvidarla,

Mi alma no da razón.

Ah, ah, ah, corazón espinado.

Ah, ah, ah, cómo me duele el amor.

That woman is killing me.

She's set thorns around my heart.

The more I try to forget her,

My soul doesn't reason.

Ah, ah, ah, thorned heart.

Ah, ah, ah, how love hurts me.'

Lis grabbed Norm's hand and dragged him out onto the sand in front of the band. She mesmerised Norm into dancing. Lis received applause for her skilled samba. The band members were smiling, and the singer continued the song, switching between Spanish and an English translation. John paid the band twenty dollars to continue with the song once more, and he and Gladys joined Lis and Norm dancing samba barefooted in the sand. Maxine sat in silence and disbelief.

At last, the band departed due to a lack of further contributions. Lis jumped down next to Norm at their usual place and said, 'Isn't it a wonderful song? It's called "Corazón Espinado" or "Thorned Heart" in English. You should hear Mana and Santana's version; it's outstanding and so captivating. I have danced to this song many times.'

Maxine's angry response came quickly, 'Yes, I can guess that, and probably with a different partner every time.' Lis shrugged her shoulders and said, 'Think what you want, but I enjoyed the song and dance, and I believe Norm did too.' Maxine looked at Norm, who was in his vacuum. He looked at the setting sun and the waves, which slowly rolled onto the beach — children were playing in the sand.

Suddenly, Norm felt a small hand, and he looked to his right between himself and Maxine. It was the little boy with the tethered iguana. The boy pulled Norm's hand and said, 'Mister, Mister, please pay to see my iguana dance.'

Norm shook his head. Lis looked behind Norm's back and said to the boy, 'I will pay you, but only if you set the iguana free. How much do you want?'

The boy was embarrassed, looked down in the sand and with a low voice said, 'I can't let him go. I love him so much.'

Lis did not give up and said, 'You can always catch another one. Now, how much do you want to let him go?'

Lis looked at Maxine, who was stone-faced with uncomfortable surprise. The boy was silent for a while and then said, 'Ok, $50 US.'

Lis looked in her bag and handed the boy a $50 note.

The little boy bent down and untied the iguana. First, the iguana didn't move, but then he touched its tail, setting it off. It ran through the sand and disappeared into the vegetation further back.

'Look,' Lis said, 'it's easy. Now he is free to go where he wants.'

Maxine and Norm said nothing, but Norm smiled at Lis.

The band reappeared, hoping for another opportunity. This time, Jack from Tank of Tiburon paid the band handsomely, asking for Corazón Espinado. He grabbed Gill's hand and nearly fell over George and Mary from Pacha II in their eagerness to get up and dance. Lis again took Norm's hand. He willingly followed her onto the sand in front of the band.

The dance went on for a while. The music changed to a slower tune. Lis pressed her body against Norm, who appeared to be in a trance, ignoring intense arousal. He looked at Maxine, who was stone-faced sitting alone trying to ignore Rick and Tanya from Third Day, who attempted a conversation through the loud singing and music. Norm saw the little boy. He had returned with another and larger tethered iguana, trying to persuade Maxine to pay for an iguana dance. Lis slowly whispered in Norm's ear, 'Puerto Escondido, my love.'

Norm and Lis returned to the table and sat down. Quietly, Maxine recited,

'O Bells of San Blas, in vain

Ye call back the Past again!

The Past is deaf to your prayer;

Out of the shadows of night

The world rolls into light;

It is daybreak everywhere.'

Maxine drove Norm back to her hotel. They did not speak. She went upstairs while Norm went to his old room in the back. In a daze of too much wine, he packed the few things he had for an early start and went to bed, pondering over his fate and why he was helpless in the hands of women. He fell asleep.

Early in the morning, the yachts and their crews left the anchorage at high tide, not waiting for Norm's roll call at eight. Lis on Amber Moon waited, but when Norm's familiar voice on Channel 22 did not appear as scheduled, she left for Puerto Escondido further south on the coast before Acapulco. Norm's body slowly left Lagoon El Pozo with the outgoing tide.

La Paz

'The only pearls left are those of wisdom; if you are lucky enough to find them.' (Unknown).

The city of La Paz at the gateway to the Sea of Cortez has a special meaning to many yachtsmen and women who travel from the West Coast of the United States to Mexico. Every year, after the hurricane season, an armada of sailing yachts join the Baja Ha-ha, a yacht rally from San Diego to Cabo San Lucas on the southern tip of Baja California. Only a few remain in Cabo, and most follow the east coast north and sail to the island Espiritu Santo. They will see the Punta Coyote lighthouse before heading west into Bahia La Paz. The yachts will arrive at Punta Prieta and navigate the La Paz Channel to reach the anchorage or the marinas. They will gather at the famous Club Cruceros, where blue water cruisers from all over the world meet before exploring the many bays and natural harbours the Sea of Cortez has to offer.

On May 3 every year, the inhabitants of La Paz celebrate the founding of the city in 1534 by the Spanish Conquistador Hernán Cortés, who gave his name to the Gulf of California as Mar de Cortés, or the Sea of Cortez. But there is not much to celebrate. The Conquistadores were brutal men with little regard for human life and an insatiable thirst for gold and silver. They argued successfully for a "Spiritual Conquest", applauded by the Roman Catholic Church. With the aid of Spanish friars, they set out to convert the vast indigenous populations to Christianity. The Conquistadores brought with them diseases that devastated the Indian people. The conversion was brought about by force.

La Paz was no exception. The first European who landed on Baja California was Fortún

Ximénez. Hernán Cortés sent two ships, the Concepción, under the command of captain and commander of the expedition, Diego de Becerra, and the San Lázaro under Captain Hernando de Grijalva, to explore the Southern Seas of the Pacific. The ships became separated, and the Concepción went alone. Onboard the Concepción, Ximénez, the navigator and second in command, led a mutiny killing Captain Becerra. They abandoned the crew loyal to the murdered captain and the Franciscan friars on the coast.

The Concepción sailed northwest, following the coast, and reached La Paz. There, Ximénez encountered the native Indians, which differed from those inhabiting the Mexican mainland. What attracted the attention of Ximénez, and his mutinous crew was that the Indians wore few clothes. They raped the women.

The Spaniards soon discovered the large pearls that the Indians found in pearl oysters common in the bay. The plundering of the Indians and the rape of the women followed. The abuse and looting caused a violent confrontation where the Indians killed Ximénez and some of his crew; the rest fled. The Concepción was eventually captured by Nuño de Guzmán, the Governor of New Galicia, who took them as prisoners.

The lust for pearls brought Sebastián Vizcaíno1. to La Paz in 1596, where he established a settlement. But the settlement was soon abandoned because of aggressive Indians and a lack of supplies. It was first in 1720 that a Mission was founded in La Paz by Jesuit fathers. By that time, the Indian population had declined and would never recover. The pearl oyster, and with them the pearls, had long gone.

John looked up from his book when Gladys entered their sitting room.

'What are you reading about?' she asked.

'I'm preparing myself for our trip to Baja California Sur. I can see us lazying around in the sun visiting the Sea of Cortez, Cabo, and La Paz on our Hallberg-Rassy 45 yacht. I thought that I should study the history of La Paz, but it's depressing reading,' John answered.

Gladys looked at John and said, 'You are quick. Have you already found a suitable yacht?'

John looked at his wife with excitement and said, 'Yes, there is one for sale in Nuevo Vallarta in Banderas Bay. It's on the hard in a boatyard in a place called "La Cruz de Huanacaxtle". It has been there for a while. It has just been listed.'

Gladys looked at John and made a defensive comment. 'So, it is one of those left behind in "the boatyard of broken dreams"?'

'I assume so,' John answered. 'But it can only mean a better price. Funny you say that. I just spoke to Jim, and he said the same. He suggested the boat is loaded with cocaine.'

Gladys suddenly felt for her husband and said, 'Don't worry about that. I will check with the agency before we leave.'

'I thought you would,' John replied with a smile.

Encouraged by the appearance of Gladys, John continued. 'Please sit down and listen. These Spanish Conquistadores were something.'

Gladys sat down next to John. He was happy to have a listener and continued, 'A fellow historian, Charles Chapman, wrote in 1920 in the Quarterly Historical about Vizcaíno: "In his voyage up the coast from Acapulco he lost fifty men by desertion, and one of the friars left the expedition because of illness. Crossing to the lower end of Baja California, he came, apparently about the middle of August, to the site which Becerra and Cortés had visited before him. Because the Indians received him so peacefully, he gave it the name La Paz (Peace), which it has retained ever since."'

'Is that it?' Gladys asked, disappointed.

'No, there is more. Be patient. Just listen.' John continued, 'He encountered terrific storms but weathered them. They came to a place where the Indians invited the Spaniards to come ashore. So, Vizcaino landed forty-five men. All went well until a Spanish soldier inconsiderately struck one of the Indians in the breast with the butt of his arquebus. In consequence, there was a fight in which some of the Indians were killed. As a boatload of Spaniards returned to their ship, the Indians fired arrows at them from the shore. One man was hit in the nose, which resulted in a commotion upsetting the boat. Dressed in heavy leathern armour, nineteen men drowned, and only five escaped by swimming.'

John looked at Gladys, who appeared bored. She moved as if she was ready to get up and walk away.

'You have no patience. It is getting better — just wait,' John explained, worried that he would lose his audience.

'Now listen to this: "Over time, this event became magnified in the telling, reaching the proportions of a pretty good legend. The story was told that a certain Don Lope, a page of the viceroy, besought the hand of Doña Elvira. The latter at length promised to marry him, provided he could replace a certain magnificent pearl she had lost. Consequently, Don Lope joined Vizcaino's expedition. He was one of the men who landed where the battle with the Indians was fought and was indeed the one who caused it. He saw a pearl that would suit Doña Elvira and seized it from the lips of a chieftain's daughter. His action brought on the battle but also the enforced abandonment of the province. But Don

Lope was well content, for he won his bride — and then she confessed she had not lost any pearl at all.'"

'Isn't that hilarious?' John asked while looking at Gladys.

Gladys looked unimpressed and said, 'It's of no surprise to me. Most people I know in the agency and elsewhere are like that.'

John shrugged his shoulders. He knew his wife did not share his enthusiasm for history. After all, as an academic, John had worked all his life in history departments at universities. Gladys had always said that he looked as grey and dusty as his books. But somehow, she always remembered what he read to her.

A couple of weeks later, Gladys and John flew to Puerto Vallarta. The yacht agent picked the couple up at the airport and drove them to La Cruz de Huanacaxtle, less than an hour's drive away. It was a new marina, now generally referred to as La Cruz.

Gladys and John had previously sailed in Mexico and many times to Banderas Bay onboard their yacht "Sunset Dreaming". A couple of years ago, they decided to sail across the Pacific along the "Coconut Milk Route". They sold their boat in New Zealand. Since then, John had second thoughts and started to look for another boat. He had been retired for a while, but Gladys still worked part time in DEA, the Drug Enforcement Agency. She had attempted retirement many times, but was brought back because of her experience, skills, and knowledge. This time, Gladys had made up her mind. She was going to retire.

The agent, named Mike, led them through a steel gate to a large, concreted area. There were a few boats for repair at the boatyard. The boatyard manager came out from his office, greeting Gladys and John and the agent from Nuevo Vallarta. He introduced himself as Will.

John looked around but could not see any Hallberg-Rassy boats or any boats for sale at all. Will guided them into a large repair hall, and there it was. The hull looked polished and fresh. Coats of antifouling paint had been applied below the waterline.

The boat was dismasted. The mast was on the ground alongside the hull. John was utterly taken aback when he saw the yacht. He turned his head and looked at Gladys, who did not show any emotions at all.

'Here it is,' Will said with a smile.

They all climbed up a ladder and went into the cockpit. Gladys immediately went below, followed by the three men. After looking around, she gave a satisfied nod towards John, who was still in a state of shock and admiration. The look on his face said everything, which the agent noted. John was not good at the principles of camel trading, so he wisely left it to Gladys.

Gladys and Mike sat in the cockpit and discussed all the interior details, while Will and John were on their knees in the engine room. They came up and inspected the teak deck. John wrote with great energy all his observations in a notebook. Finally, they looked through the sail wardrobe, laid out on the concrete floor in the hall by staff.

Will explained that the yacht had been left in the marina, and the owners, a Swedish couple, had disappeared. He believed they were somewhere overseas, probably back in Sweden. They did not pay the marina fees, and after three years, the marina management sold the yacht to recover what they were owed. Up to this point, they had not discussed the price. John expected Gladys to make a move, but she did not. He looked at her several times but only got a stern look back. John shut up and waited, but he did not find it easy. They agreed with Will and Mike to return tomorrow and go through the papers, including the new owner's certificate.

Outside the boatyard, John said, 'I didn't even see the name of the boat. Did anyone?'

Gladys nodded and said, 'It is called Miss Molly.'

She looked sternly at John and swiftly continued. 'It was painted on the back!'

John looked confused, and Mike laughed.

Gladys went straight to the marina office and left the three men in the boatyard. She asked the receptionist, a young Mexican girl, 'What is the monthly marina fee for a 45-foot yacht?'

Mike drove Gladys and John to their hotel in Nuevo Vallarta, promising to be back tomorrow at nine.

In their room, the first thing John asked was, 'Why didn't you give him an offer?'

Gladys looked at John like a mother looking at a naughty child and said, 'There is no reason. The boat will not go anywhere, and you and I must discuss this carefully before I make an offer.'

With a sigh, John sat down on a sofa and asked, 'Do you know anything that I don't?'

Gladys sat down next to him and answered, 'It is always the same, I have done my homework while you have had your nose in old books.'

John called the reception and ordered two margaritas. The couple sat on the balcony, watching the bay and the setting sun. John could not control his impatience anymore and asked in a low voice, 'What is that you know?'

Gladys looked at John and slowly said, 'The debt accrued is only three times $6500 plus interest, so the marina is making a killing. Remember, it was listed for $310,000. We will only pay $240,000 and not a cent more. The yacht's ownership has been transferred to the marina by Mexican law, and they are banking on the fact that the couple will not return and make a claim. There is a reason for this. The yacht had been monitored for drug smuggling and was probably full of cocaine. The Mexican authorities had been waiting for someone to pick it up and sail it to the US. The agency is deeply involved in the operation. They lost their patience, and now we are the guinea pigs to sail it back. The agency hopes we will be intercepted along the way. If that happens, they will swiftly move in.'

John took a large gulp of his Margarita and looked at his wife in disbelief. 'You said guinea pigs?'

Gladys nodded and harshly said, 'If you want the boat, you better get used to it.'

Gladys somewhat regretted her statement, patted John on his cheek, and smiled. John took another large gulp of his margarita.

'By the way,' Gladys said, 'I have already agreed to the price with the agency. The marina has no choice.'

John felt a sudden relief because he knew the boat would be his. Now he knew why Gladys carried an extra hard plastic suitcase and why they were whisked through the airports; she was still at work.

Gladys, John, Mike, and Will met up in the boatyard manager's office the following day. Gladys and John reached a final agreement at the price Gladys had offered. John ordered more work on the boat, primarily with the sails, navigational equipment, and automatic steering system. After three days, the work was completed to Gladys and John's satisfaction, and the boat was moved out of the repair hall. The riggers went to work inspecting the standing and running rigging. John was impressed because the yacht had two furled headsails, a genoa and a jib, and a furled mainsail. He knew well that to sail this yacht would be easier than sailing Sunset Dreaming.

Gladys organised the paperwork with registrations of radios, EPIRB, and the vessel itself. She tried to calm John down, explaining that it would take weeks. The outstanding issue was the choice of insurance. But with the boat in the water, they could move in and enjoy marina life.

To their surprise, several cruisers they had met before were there. Within a short time, guests arrived at their yacht asking for permission to come on board for an inspection. John complained about the name "Miss Molly" and had suggested to Gladys that maybe they should change the name.

'Too late,' Gladys declared. 'I have already submitted the registration forms with the name Miss Molly.'

'Good golly Miss Molly,' John said with disappointment.

The names he had in mind were "Joshua Slocum", "Admiral Pestkop", or "The Golden Hawk". None of these boat names had appealed to Gladys. John settled down and accepted Miss Molly. After all, he thought, it's a female name.

John had his nose into every space on the boat looking for drugs, but he found none. Gladys looked at him smilingly and shook her head a little. She had several communications with the agency using her SAT phone. John tried to listen to Gladys' conversations but found nothing out of the ordinary. Sitting in the cockpit, admiring the modern rigging, he looked forward to going sailing. Below, he and Gladys were impressed by the space and comfort. She, too, was looking forward to going sailing.

John was on his stomach searching the space under the bunks aft. He had piled up cans with teak oil, silicone glue cartridges and a good collection of spare parts for the engine when he suddenly cried with excitement. Gladys came into the cabin to look. To her surprise, John, still with his head under the bunk, held out a new bottle of whisky, a 12-Year-Old Scotch whisky called "The Isle of Skye".

'There is more in here,' John said with excitement and pulled out a cardboard box.

As he moved it out, he found something in the box that had leaked.

'Gladys,' John said, 'do you mind helping me with this one?'

Gladys got hold of the box, but it fell apart, and a syrupy juice ran over John's chest.

'Yuck,' he cried and crawled quickly out of the confined space.

John stood with a reproachful look on his face, trying to remove the stuff with his hand. Gladys looked in the box and said, 'It is full of leaking cans of pineapple. Go and change your shirt.'

Comfortably on the sofa with a clean shirt, John was looking at the bottle of whisky with admiration and some excitement. Gladys shared his excitement and said, 'Never mind the pineapple; it's in the bin, but the whisky looks nice. We will have a taste this afternoon, not before.'

John looked disappointed but knew if Gladys had not regulated his alcohol intake, he would have been in trouble by now.

'Is there anything more in there?' Gladys asked. John shook his head. 'No, but I have to clean up the mess.'

After two weeks of preparation, Gladys and John left La Cruz. It was a big day when they sailed away in their newly bought Hallberg-Rassy 45. The yacht did not disappoint, and in a fresh westerly wind, they tacked out of Banderas Bay, passing close to Punta Mita on their starboard side. It was about 70 nautical miles to Isla Isabela, where they would anchor for the night.

John had no intention of letting the wheel go or to activate the autopilot. He enjoyed the steering and the trimming of the sails. They smoothly ran seven knots.

Gladys sat among her pillows protected in the cockpit, scanning the ocean with her binoculars.

'We have only one boat following us. It's one of those expensive fast motor yachts of which there were many around. She has been on our tail since Punta Mita. She could easily catch up with us, but she keeps the same distance. We better watch out.'

Gladys went below and made a call on her SAT phone. On returning, she sat down and said, 'I am sorry to say, but the Mexicans are tracking the motorboat that follows us. They have placed a beacon onboard. But the agency said they would probably follow us, expecting us to go to the US, eventually.'

Gladys had another look and said, 'John, don't be anxious; we will just ignore the boat and enjoy the anchoring at Isla Isabelle.' John looked nervously at Gladys but said nothing.

Miss Molly arrived at Isla Isabela before sunset, and they anchored on the south side close to an ancient caldera with two impressive rock spires, but not so close that the breakers would bother them. There were two other yachts on anchor there. Gladys watched the motor yacht arriving, passing them further out, heading for the east side anchorage further north. John was relieved to see the motor yacht go somewhere else. He went below and came up with two glasses, ice cubes and the bottle of The Isle of Skye he had retrieved from below the bunk.

Gladys had no time for a drink; she was busy setting up electronic wiring and several gadgets along the rail and at the stern, where it was easy to access their yacht from a dinghy. John was watching while sipping on his drink but was quiet. Eventually, Gladys joined him.

After a pre-prepared dinner from La Cruz, they went to bed. John could not sleep. It was probably the fresh air and the whisky, but eventually, he did. He woke up at sunrise when the early sun shone through the windows. He got up, and in his night shorts, went up on the deck and looked forward. The sea was calm. Something caught his eye along the rail a bit ahead. He went out to investigate. He woke Gladys with a cry, 'Oh no!'

Gladys got up in the cockpit and asked, 'What is wrong?'

'You have killed two frigate birds and a cormorant, what a mess. They probably wanted to sit on the rail during the night, and your gadgets executed them instantly. In their dying hour, they have been crapping all over the deck.'

'Just clean up the mess. I will make breakfast,' Gladys said and went below.

Gladys came up in the cockpit showered and fresh. She served the breakfast while John was still in his night shorts. He had tried to get the blood and bird shit off his hands but made a mess of it. Gladys looked at him and said, 'Are you going to clean up for breakfast?'

John said nothing but slipped below for a much-needed wash.

After breakfast, they both enjoyed a cup of coffee in the sunny, calm weather. Gladys asked, 'So, what're your plans?'

John looked bewildered. 'My plans?' he answered.

'Yes, what do you have in mind?'

John gave Gladys a strange look but then composed himself and said, 'There are 264 nautical miles to La Paz from here. It will take three days even if we motor all the way. We could go to Mazatlan. It's about 90 miles; then it is 220 miles from there to La Paz. Either way, we are up for a three-day trip. Let me check the weather report before I make up my mind. Do you have a plan?'

'No, yours are fine. Just let me know when you have made up your mind.'

John was puzzled. He had no idea what was going on. He went below and called the two other cruisers and asked them if they had a weather report. The answers were unanimous: after lunch, the wind will be picking up from the southeast, and both cruisers were heading for La Paz.

'That settles that,' John said to Gladys, 'we are out of here and motor on to La Paz until the wind picks up.'

John would rather be sailing than sitting on an anchorage where they had been before. Gladys agreed.

John started the engine and got the anchor up. They passed the two-spired caldera well clear of the rocks. John looked ahead but could not see the luxury motor yacht they thought had anchored there for the night. It was gone. John asked Gladys whether she knew where it was, but she just shrugged her shoulders.

The weather report was spot-on. The wind picked up after

lunchtime, and John set all the sails. Miss Molly was flying. The wind increased to twelve knots, and John reefed the genoa. Miss Molly quickly came up to eight knots overground. At sunset, the wind died to near nothing, and they motored all night. They shared the helmsman's duty, although the autopilot was faithfully steering the boat. The following morning, the wind picked up, and they had a comfortable sail northward. John suggested splitting up the trip to La Paz, going to Los Frailes for the night, and then to Muertos for the last night before entering Bahia La Paz. Gladys nodded and smiled at John, who asked, 'I thought that you were in a hurry to get to La Paz.'

'No,' Gladys answered, 'I prefer it the slow way.'

John gave Gladys a naughty smile.

Gladys called Palmira and booked a berth. She preferred the marina La Paz, but it was packed. Giving it a second thought, Gladys told John that it would probably be better for them to stay in Palmira. She did not explain, which John did not expect.

John slowly motored Miss Molly through the La Paz Channel and entered Marina Palmira. Staff were waiting for them, waving from the dock. John got Miss Molly into the berth, and they moored safely. They thanked the staff members and all the cruisers who came running from everywhere to give a hand.

The following morning, Gladys and John walked to Marina La Paz to join the coffee hour at Club Cruceros. The place was full of people. Several fellow cruisers recognised Gladys and John from before; they were delighted.

The talk was not about sailing or pleasant anchorages, but the latest news.

John sat on a bench reading from a newspaper to Gladys, who was only mildly interested. 'Teodoro García Simental was arrested on January 12, 2010, by Mexican Federal Police in a luxury home complex named Fidepaz, located in La Paz, Baja California Sur. He was arrested together with an individual by the name of Diego Raymundo Guerrero García. Both men are believed to be members of a criminal organisation known as the Tijuana Cartel and later allied with the Sinaloa Cartel.'

'Listen to this,' John said, to maintain Gladys' attention because she was chattering to a lady opposite. 'El Teo, as Teodore was called, was involved in trafficking marijuana and methamphetamine to the US. He is known for boiling his rivals in barrels of lye in what has become known as Pozole, or the Mexican stew.'

Gladys returned to her conversation with the lady across.

A fellow cruiser came to John's aid and talked about the arrest.

'Would you believe this? They came in onboard a luxury motor yacht a couple of nights ago and moored here in the marina on the dock further out. They walked through here and disappeared in large black trucks waiting for them. I am glad that I was asleep.'

John nodded and wondered what Gladys knew.

Before lunch, Gladys and John walked back along the Malecon towards Marina Palmira. They recognised the sculptures, especially the one with the man in a paper boat. John loved that one and asked Gladys to take a photo of him next to the statue. She took a picture but pointed out that she had done that three times before. They stopped at a small supermarket to buy provisions, which they carried in small backpacks.

Sweating, they dragged their backpacks, which now felt heavier than when they left the supermarket. John and Gladys unlocked themselves through the gate to the dock. Every dock had a gate that required a key to open. With Gladys in front, the couple found the side dock where Miss Molly was moored. She put the backpack down and looked at John, who was approaching her.

'We have had a visitor,' Gladys whispered.

'How do you know that?' John asked.

'Don't worry — believe me, I know. Just wait here and be quiet.'

Gladys carefully jumped on board and began to search the cockpit. She checked all locks before moving forward along the cabin. Nothing escaped her attention. Suddenly, she got up and slowly walked forward and back to the cockpit on the other side. She stopped halfway and looked at the cabin roof.

Back in the cockpit, she looked at John and said, 'You can come onboard now.'

John obeyed and handed both backpacks to Gladys. They both went below with their bags of groceries.

John sat down on the sofa and asked, 'Now, what was that all about?'

Gladys started to unpack the groceries and said, 'Wait a bit. Let's pack the groceries out and sit down. Let's have a glass of wine, even if it's early.'

After a while, the couple sat down, each with a glass of wine. Gladys had regretted her suggestion of a glass of wine because she knew it would never end with just one drink for John. *But so what?* she thought, *He will go to sleep.*

'John,' Gladys said, 'there has been a person onboard.'

'How do you know?' John asked.

Gladys ignored the question and calmly said, 'Two small holes have been drilled into the cabin roof, one on each side.'

John did not give up that easily and asked, 'Why on earth would anybody drill small holes through the cabin roof?'

'Sometimes you appear rather naive,' Gladys said. 'They are looking for drugs.'

Gladys got up, jumped over on the dock, and said, 'Wait here. I will be back.'

Gladys disappeared along the dock, through the gate and into the marina office.

A few minutes later, she was back in the cockpit.

'One service person has been onboard. He waxed and polished the cabin roof. The office knows who it is. He used to come around asking for work,' Gladys said.

John was not holding back and swiftly said, 'Let's get his name and find him.'

'Don't be silly. We will do no such thing.' Gladys responded.

'No, we have to get the boat up on the hard in Marina Don Jose,' Gladys continued.

John looked confused and said, 'I don't understand.'

'Get your electric hand drill and an eight-millimeter drill,' Gladys asked.

John disappeared below and returned with the drill. Gladys climbed forward, looked for the place where a hole had previously been drilled. She pulled the mainsail down, so it was hanging over the rail. Gladys crept underneath. John followed. Gladys said, 'I don't want anyone to watch this.'

She quickly drilled a hole in the cabin roof and carefully pulled the drill out. She shook the powder from the drill into a small plastic bag.

'Let's go below,' Gladys said and pushed John in front of her.

Gladys placed a small plastic kit box on the cabin table. She took a small bottle and pipetted a small amount of fluid into the plastic bag with the drill powder. The fluid immediately changed colour from being clear to deep violet.

'Look,' she said, and showed it to John, 'it's cocaine — the roof is full of it.'

John sat down and asked, 'What are we going to do?'

'Now listen,' Gladys said, 'we can't stay here. While we are away, someone might take the boat away. We get it on the hard in the Abaroa, or the Don Jose Marina, asking them to change the shaft gland to a packing-less shaft seal as you wanted. I will inform the agency. Please go up and fill the hole with white putty.'

John did what she told him.

Gladys made a couple of phone calls on her SAT phone and booked an emergency haul out. The couple sailed Miss Molly to Marina Don Jose and were quickly hauled out with the excuse of a leaky gland. Safely on the hard, they left Miss Molly in the hands of the marina. They found a taxi, and Gladys told the driver,

'Casabuena Bed and Breakfast, 3065 Belisario Dominguez.'

John had no idea where they were going, but it was not far from the marina.

The following morning, a rented vehicle arrived at Casabuena, and Gladys was handed the key. She dragged John out of bed, and they drove to Cabo San Lucas. Gladys found the resort she was looking for, and they moved into a self-catered flat overlooking Bahia San Lucas.

They spent a month in the flat, which, for John, was an unexpected ordeal. Gladys tried to comfort him, and they walked a lot and dined out at night. The Isle of Skye disappeared quickly.

One evening, they were sitting on their balcony when the SAT phone rang. Gladys answered. 'John,' she said, 'open the telly on the news.'

John jumped up, and soon the news was announced. They heard, 'Yesterday, one month after the arrest of Teodoro García Simental, alias El Teo, his younger brother and lieutenant, Manuel Garcia Simental, was arrested in the Baja California port city of La Paz. Authorities feared Manuel was planning to reignite a gang war for control of Tijuana's drug trafficking routes.'

Gladys looked at John and said, 'I think the packing-less shaft seal is installed. Maybe we should try the Mexican Pozole tonight.'

John had another idea.

1. Chapman, Charles E. 1920. Sebastian Vizcaino: Exploration of California. The Southwestern Historical Quarterly. Vol. 23, No. 4, pp. 285-301.

Mayday

I met Michael Brooks in Marina Mazatlan. My wife and I had arrived the day before, coming from La Paz on the western side of the Sea of Cortez. It had been a lazy cruise with little wind, the first test sail in our newly purchased 38-ft Hans Christian. It was not a new boat, but a sturdy second-hand one reasonably well maintained. But there is always a lot of work to get a sailboat ready to cross the Pacific Ocean. We were not in a hurry.

We went on a stroll inspecting all the boats in the dock, and there it was, a beautiful 22-ft Falmouth Cutter. The boat immediately caught my eye. I cannot explain why, but since childhood, certain sailboats will always attract my attention. It has something to do with hull shape and dimension. Most good sailboats are feminine. It's how they move or dance through the water, responding to waves and swells. There are masculine boats, like tugboats, motorboats, or motor sailors. They fight the sea like a bully in a crowded shopping centre.

'Here am I, move aside, I am strong and do not yield for any wave.'

In my home country, they have the names of Viking Gods like "Thor", "Odin", and "Freja". Beautiful sailing vessels have names like "The Swan", 'The Mermaid", or just female names like "Marie", "Martha", or simply "Sweetheart".

The Falmouth Cutter was something different. She has feminine characteristics but also some masculinity. Then, of course, it's the size. It looks comfortable for a single-hander, roomy inside and designed for nearly any weather. The rigging shows that. She was called Beluga. That's the name of a small, white, toothed whale living in the Arctic. With a good imagination, that's how she looks.

There was nobody in the cockpit, but there was a person below. I could see a man bending over his laptop. We did not want to disturb the owner. We stayed in Marina Mazatlan for a couple of days, and I was sure that we would somehow meet later.

It did not take long. Yachties passed the word for a martini-time communal drink on the main dock in front of the yacht broker's office. It is not unusual that yachties meet on the docks for drinks or so-called potlucks where food is shared. It's a type of fellowship meal.

Michael Brooks appeared as a tall, grey-bearded man in his early sixties. He presented himself as an ex-New York, Paris, San Francisco ad agency art director. After a few drinks, he added a few more titles to his CV to include ex-Navy brat, ex-Marine Corps, ex-race driver, ex-husband, and a lifelong sailor. His personality appealed to me because I could recognise myself in a few of his titles.

The afternoon progressed with laughter and small talk where everybody was interested in knowing where people came from and their histories, a never-ending conversation between yachties.

Michael told us about his hectic Madison Avenue life. In order not to end up on the endless suicide list of New York executives, he had to navigate between marriage and getting fired. Eventually, it became too much, and he headed for the open sea and the tropical isles beyond. The freedom he felt, relieving himself from life's depressing constraints, saved him, and there was no turning back. With his "beer money", he sailed to the Bahamas, the Caribbean, across the South Pacific and back to the Sea of Cortez. He was happy about the quiet life on board, writing his novels and screenplays. No regrets.

I had hoped to spend more time with Michael, but the reason for our Mazatlan trip was to fix rigging and motor problems in the local boatyard. As soon as the issues were resolved, we would return to our favourite harbour of La Paz, hoping the hurricane season would ignore us.

In late July, we passed the small Marina El Cid at the narrow entrance to Marina Mazatlan and headed northwest on the 230 NM trip to La Paz on the southeastern coast of the Californian Peninsula. It was a three-day trip.

At first, it was a lazy trip — little wind during the day and calm at night. We motored along at a steady pace. On the second day's afternoon, we could see the high coast of the Baja California coastline, a comforting sight. The autopilot steered the boat, and the engine was running softly below. We had a cup of coffee. I said to Gladys, 'Have you noticed we haven't seen a single sail out here? Where are they all?'

'Yes, you are right. We have it all to ourselves,' she answered.

I got up and sat on the helmsman's seat, looking forward. I spotted something on the horizon. I looked through the binoculars, and sure enough, there was a small sail way ahead.

'We have company!' I said to Gladys with some excitement.

Suddenly, there was a crackling sound from the VHF radio, always set on Channel 16, the emergency channel. Imbedded in the crackling noise, I heard the dreaded call.

'Mayday, Mayday, Mayday.'

I looked around, wondering where the signal came from. There was only one boat to see. I heard voices in Spanish reporting what sounded like a position. Then it changed to English. I only managed to hear half of it. Then I heard a voice finishing off saying, 'Beluga, standing by!'

I would not interfere with emergency radio traffic, but I had the creeping feeling that it was Beluga with Michael on board and straight ahead.

I grabbed the mic with hesitation and called, 'Beluga, Beluga, Beluga; this is Sunset Dreaming, over.'

After a bit of crackling, I got a response and asked, 'Beluga, are you in trouble?'

A voice fell in and out, partly disappearing in the crackle. I read that the problem was water coming in and that it was now over the floorboards. There was no pump. A mesmerising and confusing flow of other information followed. I heard, 'A fast vessel is approaching!'

I looked up, and there were no other vessels in sight. I finished the conversation,

'Beluga, Beluga, I am approaching fast from the east. I have a pump, over.'

The crackling radio stopped. Soon I had my nose in the spare parts compartment and fished out an extra pump. I rushed upon the deck where Gladys was already at the wheel, motoring as fast as Sunset Dreaming could muster.

It felt like hours before we could clearly see Beluga. A vessel appeared from the South. It turned out that the "fast vessel" was a five hatch Mexican bulk carrier approaching at a speed of approximately thirteen knots! There was communication between Beluga and the carrier named "Port Shanghai", so I stood by. Port Shanghai emitted clouds of black smoke when she put the engine in reverse. A five-hatch bulk carrier needs a long distance to stop, and she had everything going for it. Fortunately, the weather had mercy on us. It was flat calm.

Eventually, Port Shanghai ran up alongside Beluga, dwarfing the small 22-foot Falmouth Cutter. Its mast was barely halfway up to the deck. A swarm of sailors were busy getting a hose into Beluga. I heard Beluga's captain shouting, as if in complaint, but the hose came down, and in a few minutes, all water was pumped out.

Quickly, Beluga headed towards us to collect our spare pump. As I passed the pump over to a very exhausted Michael, the Mexican Coast Guard came flying in on one of their fast patrol vessels. With help from one of the officers, the pump got connected. Now there were about 100 nautical miles to the safety of La Paz, and it was getting dark. But the Mexican Coast Guard would not let us go before both Beluga and Sunset Dreaming were thoroughly inspected. I heard Beluga thanking the captain of Port Shanghai many times. Suddenly, we were alone.

We left Channel 16, and I heard Michael's story while motoring on our intended course to La Paz. On her way north, Beluga had started to take in water from an unknown source. After a while, the electric pump broke down, and Michael had to bail with a bucket. Then his tiller pilot gave up. He had to bail and steer simultaneously because there was no wind allowing him to let his windvane steer Beluga. His ordeal went on through the night and half a day until exhaustion took the best out of him, and he called Mayday. Now he had to hope that our spare pump would do the job through the night. We decided to follow Beluga closely all the way.

'You know what?' Michael said. 'The fucking pump on the bulk carrier ate all the labels from my wine collection!'

I thought it was a small sacrifice. It was clear Michael had prepared himself to meet his creator, but he decided to give life another chance. It was a brave decision.

We kept a close watch on Beluga through the night, knowing that Michael was likely to fall asleep, and he did. Beluga zigzagged towards Isla Espiritu Santo and the entrance to Bahia La Paz.

After midnight, a distressed Michael reported that our spare pump had failed. The only option Michael had left was to connect a hose from the engine cooling pump to the bilge with the risk of overheating the engine. He did that, and it worked.

At daybreak, we were happy to hear that Michael was still in good spirit. We watched Beluga sailing into La Paz and the emergency haul-out at the Abora Boatyard. Here the leak became known. It was a hose connecting the stern tube to the packing box, a commonplace for leakage because over time, ozone from the engine degrades the rubber, a silent killer. This time, death left empty-handed. Learning the lesson, we replaced our own packing gland with a modern dripless shaft seal.

Puerto Escondido

Three knocks on the hull, and a call of 'Buenos Dias, Amigo!' woke me up, just after sunrise.

A smiling face greeted me as I looked out of the cockpit. It was a Mexican man in working clothes 'Captain, do you want your boat polished today?'

I looked at him and reluctantly answered, 'You polished my boat last week!'

He went on. 'Maybe your bottom needs cleaning?'

'No, I said, it just got painted!'

'Okay, Captain, maybe some other time?'

'Yes, I replied, maybe some other time.'

I got off the bunk because I was expecting another knock.

'Due for a haircut, Sir?' — it did not eventuate.

The place is Marina La Paz, close to the tip of the Californian Peninsula, protected from the Pacific Ocean, and guarding the entrance to the Sea of Cortez, a gathering place for yachtsmen.

At the start of the North American autumn, yachts in numbers leave the coast of California, and like migrating birds, they fly south, taking advantage of the northerly winds, guiding them along the coast. They gather first at Ensenada, the entry point to Mexico, then sail further, stopping at a few anchorages on the way. For many, the rounding of the Baja California Peninsula at Cabo San Lucas is a relief, and just a short sail from their primary destination, the safe anchorage of La Paz. Here many yachtsmen settle-in either on the anchorage or, for those who can afford the cost, in Marina La Paz, the headquarters of "Club Cruceros,", or in Marina Palmira further out. For many, it is the point of no return, because the route back to California is by way of Hawaii, avoiding the northerly winds and coastal currents.

The crew on the southbound yachts are ordinary people, married couples and returned servicemen, many scared and wounded. They are not wealthy, but simple people who found a paradise where their meagre pensions can sustain a free lifestyle. The size of the fleet represents the ups and downs of the North American economy. But they are always warmly greeted by the Mexicans.

There are also other migrating yachts in La Paz. They are serious sailors who have reached the end of a long circumnavigation. They left from here, and they arrived here. During the coffee hour at Club Cruceros, there are many voices of different nationalities. It is from yachtsmen and women who have crossed the Atlantic, sailed through the Caribbean, and finally transited the Panama Canal. They found shelter in La Paz for repairs and provisions before a Pacific crossing. One might say La Paz is the world center for yachtsmen, sailors, adventures, or people who want to get away from it all. They are among equals and find comfort in the real generosity of ordinary Americans, or Gringos, and Mexicans alike.

Many yachtsmen and women will stay here, live on their boats, and explore the Sea of Cortez and its many natural harbours. With the threat of an approaching hurricane season, many will pack up and sail to the northern end of the Sea of Cortez. Here, they will slip their boats on land and jump in their campers, enjoying the outdoors during spring and summer. By November, they will be back in La Paz, greeted as long-lost friends.

Another cohort of people approaches by air. Like vultures high in the sky, they fly into LAX, and descend on boatyards from Seattle to San Diego, scavenging on yachts for sale. These people have left Melbourne, Sydney or elsewhere for an extended vacation, expecting to sail their purchase leisurely back along the coconut milk trail. Many travel even further to the Florida yacht heaven of Fort Lauderdale, lured by the cheap offer of decommissioned yachts and catamarans from the Caribbean charter business. These boats are usually not suitable for long ocean voyages but are weekend cruisers. They are cheaply built for easy dismantling, without a keel and mast, to fit into a shipping container. On these yachts, it is best for your safety to stay in sight of your home harbour. The attraction of this trade is for gamblers and the inexperienced, willing to risk their lives for the prospect of an extended vacation, and a small profit when eventually arriving off Botany Bay. Others search far and wide for the best oceangoing yachts available for the budget at hand. And there are quite a few. Guided by yacht sales agents, people descend on La Paz boatyards, which harbours rows of boats left behind by broken marriages, financial ruin, or death. They are sold to recover the debt to the boatyards, and, with luck, real gems can be found.

Before long, there is a hub of activity, preparing yachts for voyages in the Sea of Cortez, along the coast of Mexico, and beyond. The center of activity is at Club Cruceros, where everybody meets, shares camaraderie, drinks coffee, and collects mail. It is the place to discuss weather reports, boat improvements, and spare parts. There are no limits to the availability of experts; it's the heaven of pros and cons. In tradition, the bench outside the clubhouse is often referred to as the "Liar's Bench"!

For many on anchor or in the marinas, the most important event of the day is the morning roll call or "net", organised by the members of Club Cruceros. A volunteer, usually the same every day, will, as "net controller", call all boats on a VHF frequency at eight o'clock sharp, announcing the roll call. One by one, listening yachts will call in by briefly stating their boat name. Then the net controller will go through an established schedule, starting with the most important. 'Any medical emergencies?' and then a suit of points addressing various needs.

Yachts will participate with comments and helpful information. For people new to boating, these calls are a lifeline, an introduction to the general La Paz sailing community. At the end of the session, there will be more calls from the participating yachts, announcing events of interest, such as fundraisers, parties on docks, or music entertainment in the adjacent restaurants. Some calls would be like this: 'Alcohol Anonymous is having a meeting tonight. Those who want to participate, please call on channel 68 after the net!'

A flourish of activity of inter-ship calls usually follows the net, many displaying the plethora of bizarre boat names: 'Cat Miaow, Cat Miaow this is Two Can Play — over'. Followed by, 'Two Can Play, Two Can Play, this is Cat Miaow, please go to channel 69.'

One can only wonder what they are doing.

During January, many boats will sail south to Banderas Bay and join "The Pacific Puddle Jump", organised by the editor of the yacht magazine, "Latitude 38". The magazine is printed on relatively cheap paper with no glossy covers and content and distributed for free. A lot of the content is written by the cruising fraternity, providing stories of exploits, and family sailing.

In Banderas Bay, there are three marinas, the main one in Puerto Vallarta itself, one just north of the harbour, Nuevo Vallarta, and one at the small town of La Cruz on the northern shore. Here, the level of activity is high because Puerto Vallarta is an official exit port for boats leaving for overseas destinations. Yachts of many nationalities will make their last preparations, some seeking crew for the passage to French Polynesia. All will eventually confront officials with their papers, told to leave the harbour within twenty-four hours, and finally head out for the open ocean. There is no fixed departure date, but it is wise to go before the onset of the official hurricane season on April 1, and most do.

What governs the departure date is the weather report. Everybody discusses the weather patterns of the Eastern Pacific, but only one thing counts — a morning weather report from California. Yachtsmen wait patiently on the morning net on single-sideband HF radio. A dedicated retired meteorologist provides this appreciated service as a charity for the Pacific Puddle Jump. Others buy the service of so-called "Weather Routers". They sell their products like a Haruspex wandering the ancient streets of Athens, telling fortunes by studying the open guts of animals. They never admit that any weather report is only reasonably accurate for three days; from thereon it is up to chance!

On one morning, the weather report was unexpectedly delayed for an hour. After the usual roll call and general schedule, the net controller was scrambling for entertainment. His choice was the origin of the boat names belonging to the listening yachtsmen. Names like "Wrinkle Bottom", "Scarlet Muse", "Chardonnay", "Done Dreaming", and "Tarzoom the Shame of the Jungle", were discussed in detail, and the various reasons why particular names were selected. Nobody could provide reasonable answers. It was like asking a person why he has inked his buttocks with a pile of coal on one side, and a man with a shovel on the other.

Then the net controller turned his attention to an Australian yachtsman, known as a keen participant in the net by entertaining listeners with his admiration for his American wife, based on his innuendo of women's anatomy and Tasmania.

'Don, the name of your boat is Buena Vista. Why did you give it that name?'

A long pause followed, then in broad Australian, 'Well mate, it was written on the back when I bought it!'

Close to April, the most reluctant boats eventually leave their harbour. For many, it's the first time they have ever sailed the open ocean. The yachts do not leave all at the same time, but organised HF nets keep yachts in touch. The chatter on these nets reveals a nervousness on some yachts, where even minor problems make the crew discuss whether it would be best to return. It is "the point of no return"!

"If you go back, you will lose face," is a common phrase provided by less understanding onlookers. Others will be more philosophical, use expressions like Julius Caesar when he crossed the Rubicon River: "Alea iacta est!", or in Jean-Paul Sartre's version, "Les jeux sont faits!". The die is cast — it truly is the point of no return.

A yacht with a hired crew, or crew member, may face serious challenges. Sailing experience is a rare commodity, but young adventurous volunteers are many. Within a week spent in a confined space, on night watch, and with seasickness, the dream of smooth adventurous sailing has faded away. The surprise of a tropical squall may have been a near-death experience. Before long, the new crew member is unable to perform even the most straightforward task, lying restlessly on the bunk. Complaints will be many, and hateful arguments may follow where murder is an option. The hasty departure of the hired crew by air from the first port of call proves this point. Only a few will last. Surprisingly, the best crew is a family with young children.

All must face that, on average, a passage from Mexico to the Marquesas, where Hiva Oa is the first port of call, will take twenty-four days. The type of yacht does not determine the length of the voyage, it is the weather you encounter and your attention to navigation.

The weather dangers are tropical squalls. They seem to follow you around. Massive Cumulus clouds rise high in the sky, bringing strong winds, rain, and lightning. You wish to avoid the squalls but cannot. You must keep your course. The best thing to do is to reduce sail when needed, especially at night. After crossing the Equator, yachts meet the doldrums, and the trans-equatorial current forcing them westwards. Boats must cross the Equator before 130 degrees west to reach the Marquesas. Otherwise, they may risk their boats on the shallow coral reefs of the Tuamotus Islands. This prospect is real, especially at night. The Tuamotus is a myriad of low-lying islands and coral reefs. They are not likely to show up on the radar.

Most yachtsmen will not see any boats at all before landfall. After twenty-four days or so, the crew will get the first scent of flowers, earth, and land. It is close to a transcendental experience, bringing many to tears. After this, most will never be the same again. They will be sailors, real sailors, always on the lookout for a Puerto Escondido, or hidden port, of which there are many in Mexico.

Cumulus

The sea was grey, and cumulus clouds were building up like massive towers stretching high up in the sky. They were black and grey. None were close, and in the distance, there was rain and lightning, but no sound. The wind was constantly changing direction.

'Is the weather going to get worse?' a young woman asked the captain.

'Maybe, maybe not,' he answered. 'But we must be prepared. It's typical tropical weather; we keep our course trying to avoid the clouds.'

The main was a storm-sail. The furling genoa was out, but ready to be reduced if needed. The horizon was eerie.

'It's strange to think', said the young woman, 'that yesterday the sky was blue, and we celebrated our passage of the Equator.'

The captain looked firmly at her and said, 'Go below and get us some fruit and water. There are apples in the drawer.'

He then addressed the crew, 'Guys, check below that all seacocks are locked, and get on your wet weather gear. Remember lifejackets and security lines.'

The yacht continued tagging along as the wind changed. After all, there was nothing more the captain could do; they were 210 nautical miles from the Marquesas Islands in the west and far further from the coast of South America.

Darkness fell, and the cook called the crew for dinner. The captain finished his meal on deck, hooked onto the safety line. Below, all dirty plates were in the sink, and the cook had opened the seacock to wash the dishes.

In a flash of a second, a massive blow hit the yacht, forcing it on its side. The wind was howling, the rain pouring down. A wave came over the rail, too much for the drainage, washing two crew overboard and flushing into the galley. The noise was terrifying. The captain released the autopilot and grabbed the wheel, trying to steer up against the wind. Desperately he shouted, 'Start the engine.'

But nothing happened. He looked below and saw cabin boards floating and the cook trying to close a valve. A geyser of water came out of the sink, sending the plates flying.

The young woman in wet weather gear appeared in the hatch.

'Hold the sheet in the cleat and ease out as I winch the genoa in,' the captain shouted.

Another large wave broke over the cockpit and washed the captain overboard. After a time, which felt like hours, the captain reappeared in the cockpit after pulling himself up using the safety line. The young woman was at the helm, steering the boat downwind. The engine started, and the cook looked out, shouting, 'Where is the crew?'

The captain looked at the cook, quietly saying, 'We must pray to our holy mother. We lost two young men with little chance of finding them.'

'No, not yet,' the young woman said. 'I pressed the "man overboard" button so we will turn around when ready.'

Marquesas

The 40-foot yacht, Sunset Dreaming, with John and Gladys onboard, cruised leisurely in the south-easterly direction. When they crossed the Equator, there was hardly any wind, and they had to motor for hours on end. Then the weather changed as large cumulus clouds filled the horizon, bringing windy squalls of driving rain, thunder, and lightning. Sailing became exhausting, but John and Gladys worked well together throughout the day and night. Eventually, the weather stabilised, and for the last three days, they had experienced a steady ten to fifteen knots easterly. It was now twenty days since they left Banderas Bay in Mexico and John expected that with this wind, they would reach the Marquesas Islands in four days. During the passage, they had seen no boats at all, but they had kept communications on HF-radio with other yachts sailing the same route.

Gladys and John rested comfortably on blue marine cushions fitted to both benches on either side of the cockpit. Extra pillows allowed the two yachties to lean against the coaming. John could observe the functioning of the windvane at the stern, which steered their yacht. Occasionally, he could see large Spanish mackerels surfing in the wake rolling behind. Some days, they dragged a trolling lure behind the boat to catch fish. They often caught Spanish mackerels, but they both preferred the colourful dolphin fish, Mahi-mahi. The problem with fishing was that they always caught huge fish which was a battle to get onboard and kill. One fish would feed them for days, and a lot eventually had to be thrown overboard because their fridge-freezer was small.

'I am really looking forward to seeing land again,' Gladys said while half reading a book. She continued. 'Did you know, John, that there are cannibals in the Marquesas?'

John looked up from his book, glanced at Gladys, and said, 'Where did you get that idea? There may have been cannibals sometime in the past, but not now.'

John again turned his attention to his book. But Gladys continued. 'Well, I am reading here that a Mr. W. D. Rubinstein believes it is considered a great triumph among the Marquesan's to eat the body of a dead man; they call the roast a "long pig".' Gladys looked at John as if she was evaluating a piece of steak in a gourmet butcher shop. She continued her story. 'Rubinstein says that the natives treated captives with great cruelty. They broke their legs to prevent them from escaping before being eaten. He even says that bodies of women were in great demand — maybe we should have considered another destination?'

Gladys gave John a worried look.

'Too late now,' John muttered with little concern for Gladys' worries.

But Gladys did not give up that easily and continued. 'Did you know that it is not illegal to eat human flesh? It's when you kill someone and then consume the body, you will be convicted of murder. There is a story in my magazine about a man, who in 1988 ate the flesh of another person in public. He legally ate a canapé of donated human tonsils in Walthamstow High Street, London. A year later, he publicly ate a slice of a human testicle in Lewisham High Street. Then, when he tried the same act at the Pitt International Galleries in Vancouver, the police confiscated the testicular hors d'oeuvre. In the end, the police dropped the charge of publicly exhibiting a disgusting object. I will give him credit for his determination because he finally ate a piece of a human testicle on the steps of the Vancouver Courthouse.'

John looked up from his book with a sigh and said, 'It will not be a surprise to me. Think about all those cooking shows with celebrity gourmet chefs; they always come up with something exotic to eat — everything from rare rodents to cockroaches and reptiles, so why not human flesh? Remember the movie, in which an English gourmet wanted his meal to be that of someone's soul —not much meat in that one. But I read a historical account of the incident which was the source of inspiration for Herman Melville's novel "Moby Dick". It happened not far from Marquesas. In 1820, a sperm whale rammed and sank the whaling ship "Essex of Nantucket". The crew got into three small boats. They knew the Marquesas were not far away but chose to sail east towards South America, much further away. They had heard that there were cannibals on the islands, a largely spurious tale. I think it is an irony of proportion because many of the crew died, and in despair the survivors resorted to cannibalism, eating the corpses. It took them three months to reach land. Now, I think I'm looking forward to a big steak when we come to Hiva Oa!'

Two days off the Marquesas, the weather changed to overcast and variable winds, sometimes with a gust of rain. Gladys and John on Sunset Dreaming quickly adjusted to the changing conditions. Sleep was fitful and scarce.

They approached the Marquesas Island of Hiva Oa at midnight. It was pitch black and raining, but they had smelled the island hours before. It was a sweet scent of flowers and earth which brought Gladys to tears. It was the first time she had been on a yacht on an ocean passage for such a long time. John was also captivated by the experience but didn't show it. It was when they heard a rooster's call that he became a bit emotional. After all, the last few days had been exhausting, but now they could see the end of the passage. Both John and Gladys looked closely at the radar image and on their GPS plotter. They could not see the harbour but only a landmass and therefore decided to take the sails down and start the engine. Slowly, they motored on and passed well off an outcrop projecting from the island. The breakwater and the harbour now revealed themselves on the radar screen. To their surprise, the radar showed a harbour full of boats and, with a look through the binoculars, John saw many mast lights moving back and forth.

'Gladys,' he said, 'I think we must anchor outside the breakwater for the night. There are way too many boats in there!'

Gladys had a look and agreed.

'Better to be safe than sorry,' she said, a bit disappointed.

Outside the breakwater, they dropped the anchor and found a perfect hold. There was less swell than they had feared, and the couple settled down in the cockpit for a midnight drink. Now they imbibed all the exotic smells and noises from the island, but they could see nothing but the breakwater and the silhouettes of the high hills. The slight swell and the reflecting waves from the breakwater did not bother Gladys and John. John remained on deck while Gladys went below to sleep. At five, she relieved her husband for a few hours' sleep.

At sunrise, Gladys saw the island for the first time. She became overwhelmed by the smell of tropical flowers, the birdsong, and the lush green vegetation; she just sat in a trance with tears running down her cheeks. Suddenly she jumped up, rushed below yelling,

'John, John, you must come up and see this!'

She grabbed his shoulder, pushing him backwards and forwards. John looked up, ignored his drowsiness and completely numb, followed Gladys up on the deck. Gladys pointed towards the hills above the harbour and looked at John with excitement. The lush, green hills were saturated with blood acacias, plumerias and hibiscus. Their scent was overwhelming. John slowly laid his arms around Gladys and gave her a long hug, whispering into her ear, 'I understand; we made it, yes, we made it!'

During the morning, Gladys and John found a place to anchor among the many yachts inside the breakwater. It was an uncomfortable harbour because of the need to make space for the regular arrival of a supply vessel from Papeete, the capital of French Polynesia. The swell surged into the harbour, and there was no place to secure a dinghy. The usual practice under such circumstances was to drop a small anchor and then attach the dinghy to land. Competition for space was fierce, and an unfriendly yachtsman might release the mooring, allowing the dinghy to drift around by the anchor. In any case, at least one of the dinghy passengers would be wet when trying to get ashore. But everybody had to go to clear customs and immigration before being allowed into Polynesia.

Gladys did what she always did, checking out all the boats in the harbour. She recognised a couple from Marina La Cruz in Banderas Bay, yachts they had joined on the HF net. But there was one which attracted her attention. It was a large, white, aluminum luxury yacht. It looked modern and brand new, she thought. The yacht had an automatic movable stern, allowing the transfer of a large dinghy with a center console into her hull. The vessel was in sharp contrast to the much smaller cruisers. The name of the boat was Alumnus of Guernsey. Gladys thought that some wealthy, arrogant academic freak would own it. There was always a crew member shouting in broken English at neighbouring yachts, asking them to move on or risk an expensive court case if they accidentally scratched their glossy paint while on anchor. Occasionally, the rosy head of a woman popped up from below and joined the shouting in an obscure German dialect.

'John,' Gladys said pointing, 'have a look at the big one over there.'

John grabbed the binoculars and watched a short, stocky, bearded, and bald man shouting at a neighbouring yacht.

'They are tiny people on that boat; I think there are three of them. From here it looks like "Snow White and the two dwarfs", with the exception that they all seem to be at least in their late sixties,'

John chuckled, but Gladys continued, 'Having a yacht like that and then registered in Guernsey; they must be rich people, and what a nerve; they are pushing people around!' Gladys looked at the spectacle with indignation.

In the early afternoon, when the rush was less, John and Gladys got ashore and walked up the hill to the town. The road uphill was lined with flowering blood acacia's, amaryllis, and lush vegetation. Everywhere, uncatchable lean chicks were running squiggly around. One of the locals had watched John's attempt and shouted, 'If you catch one, you can have it!'

After finishing their business with customs and migration, they took a stroll through the town. They quickly realised why there was a rush in the morning; the baker had sold everything — there was not a crumb left. They visited a small museum dedicated to the famous French painter, Gaugin, who once lived on the island. Somewhat disappointed with the museum and the lack of bread, they walked back to the harbour and got onboard Sunset Dreaming for a rest.

The following day, Gladys and John were up at sunrise. Several yachts, including Alumnus of Guernsey, had left, leaving the harbour less crowded. Most of the day was spent getting fuel and water and topping up their depleted provisions. Even the baker had fresh bread available. They planned to leave Hiva Oa for a neighbouring island, Nuku Hiva, a short distance to the north.

Up in town, the couple ran into another cruiser couple, Neil, and Jenny on Pearly White. They had a coffee together, and Neil told them that there was a beautiful small bay just west of the town Taioha'e called Daniels Bay or Hakaui which he and Jenny would like to visit.

'Join us,' Neil said, 'there may be cannibals there!'

He handed John an old edition of the New York Post they had

carried with them since Banderas Bay.

'Look at page fifteen,' Jenny said excitingly.

John found page fifteen, which had an article with a big headline. "Holiday Horror on Cannibal Island: An adventurer and his girlfriend who visited a remote Pacific Island, was last night feared to have been eaten by natives."

John read on and realised that it was the Marquesas the journalist had referred to; but then Gladys snatched the paper from him.

'Let me read it,' she said without providing any apology.

A moment later, Gladys folded the paper and said, 'It was a while ago. I think it is sensationalism. I have read about it somewhere else. It was a murder committed by one of the locals who was a guide for two Germans on a catamaran. The guide murdered the man and burned him, but the woman got away. The police searched for the guide but failed to find him even when using French commandoes. Eventually, the guide handed himself in to the police. Accusing Polynesians of cannibalism has a long history, and it is usually malicious stereotyping.'

With a firm look, Gladys handed the paper back to Neil. John looked at Neil and Jenny and said, 'Sorry, Gladys always has a problem with journalists and how they twist and bend the news, but I am sure we would like to join you in Daniels Bay.'

The following morning, the two yachts, Sunset Dreaming and Pearly White, set sail for Nuku Hiva and the town of Taioha'e some 85 nautical miles to the north. The weather was favourable, and a fifteen knot easterly blew them quickly across. The high volcanic pillars of Hiva Oa disappeared behind them as the pillars of Nuku Hiva appeared ahead. At dusk, they anchored in a wide bay with black sandy beaches. Gladys noted that Alumnus of Guernsey was in the bay. No one felt any desire to go ashore, and after a good night's rest they sailed the 4 nautical miles east to Daniels Bay or Hakatea.

The picturesque Daniels Bay is surrounded by high hills and has a narrow entrance, a perfect natural harbour. Gladys and John admired the breathtaking scenery, and Gladys said, 'This place is too pretty to be the site of a murder.'

With the two yachts safely anchored, both couples motored their dinghies to the shore and walked up the dirt road to the village. They could hear goats in the hills. Gladys looked back and saw Alumnus of Guernsey sailing through the entrance of the bay. A small horse was grazing in a paddock, and there were many trees with ripe mangoes. Veggie patches, coconut, and banana trees were everywhere. Among the trees, the village of Hakaui with a few wooden houses with corrugated iron roofs appeared.

The cruisers were greeted by a fit looking muscular man with a few Polynesian tattoos on his arms and shoulders. He introduced himself as Augustine and invited the cruisers to a small roofed area with a long table with benches around. While peeling a large grapefruit, he asked where the cruisers came from and whether they would be interested in a hike to the waterfall. Soon there was a lively conversation between the two girls and Augustine, most likely stimulated by his sun tainted, muscular appearance and his charming, welcoming approach. After enjoying the grapefruit and some slices of mango, the company was on their way up to the waterfall. Augustine showed them old rock foundations from the early times of the village, which were also the foundations for many of the existing houses. There were a few ancient statues carved in volcanic rock. Only a few people were around, and Augustine explained that most had moved to Taioha'e because their children had to go to school there.

After half an hour's walk, the company arrived at a tall, narrow waterfall, spectacularly splashing down into a fresh-looking, clear pool. Following Augustine's lead, they all walked into the pool in knee-high water where he pointed at small schools of freshwater prawns swimming along the bottom. Augustine said that they were welcome to take a swim. The girls giggled; they felt tempted, but their spouses did not.

On their way back to Augustine's house, they saw the two bearded men and the rosy-faced woman from Alumnus walking up the road. Augustine invited everybody to his table and again started to peel a grapefruit for his guests. They all sat on the benches in silence because the three new guests did not appear to be interested in any conversation. All enjoyed the grapefruit, which was cool and fresh, after the long walk in the heat and humidity.

Neil invited Augustine and the three newcomers to the evenings "potluck".

'Bring some food and your own poison, and I will supplement with nibbles and some wine,' he said.

Augustine nodded, said thanks, and suggested using the green paddock in the bottom of the bay. The three newcomers had a conference in a language Gladys thought was a German dialect of some sort. One of the males turned towards Neil and said, 'Danke, wir will come!'

More yachts had arrived, and as the sun disappeared behind the hills, a crowd had assembled on the narrow beach at the green paddock. Augustine had lit a fire, and Neil ensured everybody had a drink. Most people were standing next to the fire because at that hour the mosquitoes had come out, and on the narrow beach sand flies were numerous. A lot of nibbles had arrived from the boats, including a variety of salads dishes. The evening progressed and the crowd seemed happy.

The three people from Alumnus of Guernsey sat together quietly talking to Augustine. Gladys tried to stay close to be within hearing distance. She dragged Jenny with her, but Jenny pulled the other way because of the mosquitoes. Gladys got a can of insecticide from her bag and sprayed Jenny's shoulders, arms, and legs.

'That will do it!' she said in a comforting tone.

Jenny could see that Gladys was trying to listen in to the conversation between the three Germans and Augustine and asked, nearly whispering, 'Are you trying to eavesdrop?'

Gladys smiled and gave a reluctant small nod. Now both girls were listening.

Augustine got up and left the crew members of Alumnus to themselves and their German beers. Jenny and Gladys went over to the table to get some finger food and withdrew a bit from the crowd at the fire.

'Did you hear that?' Gladys asked. 'I might be wrong, but I believe they asked Augustine for human flesh. I heard the words "La chair humaine," and the woman repeated several times in a low voice the German "Menschenfleisch". I am sure they are up to something.'

After the potluck, Neil and Jenny joined John and Gladys on Sunset Dreaming for an early nightcap. Neil and John listened to the girls when they reported their interpretation of their eavesdrop.

'I am sure you are right,' Neil said. 'I have been told that after the newspaper reports on cannibalism, many people had come to the Marquesas asking for the same thing. It is some kind of craze among European gourmets which in these days are sweeping the television channels with cooking shows. Somebody told me that in many cases it is combined with sex tourism. I can tell you that the inhabitants on these islands are fed up with it. It will be interesting to see what will happen because before we left the paddock, Augustine invited all the cruisers for goat on the spit tomorrow night if his hunt was successful. He was only asking $20 each,' John said.

Gladys and Jenny looked at each other with excitement. Gladys glanced at John and then at their two friends and thoughtfully said, 'It reminds me of the famous scene in "The Silence of the

Lambs" where Anthony Hopkins, as Hannibal Lecter, talks to Clarice and says, "I ate his liver with some fava beans and a nice Chianti!" I wonder whether we have any Fava beans and Chianti onboard?'

Early the next morning, the two couples went trekking up in the hills following a well-trotted path starting from the green paddock. Augustine had told them that the track leads up to a viewpoint from where they could see over the whole island and the neighbouring ones too. He was right. After an hour, they reached the top and sat in silence on a couple of rocks, sweating and drinking water. The view was breathtaking. On hearing a couple of gunshots in the distance and Neil said, 'I think that Augustine has been successful in his hunt.'

On their way back to their boat's hours later, they met Augustine at the green paddock setting up two big rotisserie spits. There were several bags of charcoal.

'Things went well,' he said. 'I reckon the meat will be ready around eight.'

Augustine did not speak English well, and when he ran out of words, he often changed to French in the middle of a sentence, but Gladys translated. Augustine declined John's offer to help.

At dusk, all the cruisers had gathered on the foreshore where two large spits with whole goats were roasting. On a third spit, there was a large leg with a part of a femur exposed.

The smell of roasting meat was delightful and reached the nostrils of everybody there. Augustine worked on the roast and brushed the meat with an oily solution of spices and herbs. Between brushings, he made up a series of exotic salads; one of them he called "millionaire's salad" to impress Gladys and Jenny, who had asked many questions about his cooking.

'The millionaire's salad,' Augustine explained, 'is a salad of thinly sliced rings of tender hearts of a young coconut palm, mixed with lettuce and other items, depending on my whim of the day. The salad is called the millionaire's salad because the ingredients can be expensive, but not here.'

Gladys looked at the spit with the leg with suspicion. She grabbed hold of John's arm and whispered, 'I think the leg is human. It is the same size, and look at the crispy skin — what else can it be?'

John shook his shoulders, and so did Neil. She got Jenny into her confidence, and she agreed. They were convinced it was human and were looking forward to seeing who was going to eat it.

All the cruisers had come ashore and were deep into their longdrinks, beers, and wine, when Augustine declared the meat ready. Next to him were two village women to help him. He got up on a bench and loudly chanted long sentences in Polynesian, looking up in the sky, stretching out his arms and pounded both his fists into his chest while sticking out his tongue. It was a spectacular performance when he danced and chanted loudly, like the Maori Haka from New Zealand.

Augustine jumped off the bench, walked a few steps towards the three crew members from Alumna of Guernsey, pointed at the roasted leg and said, 'Bon appétit.'

He then turned his attention to the other cruisers and pointed at the table where one of the two women had carved out the roasted goat, and said, 'C'est de la chèvre — goat — Bon appétit.'

Meanwhile, the other woman had carefully carved out meat from the leg and placed it on three nicely carved wooden plates. She handed the plates to each of the three crew members from Alumna of Guernsey. Augustine stepped back and cried, 'Please help yourself to the salads!'

Gladys and Jenny enjoyed the millionaire's salad and thin pieces of the delicious roasted goat. While eating, they now and then looked smirkingly at the three crew members who spoke to one another with low voices with a German sound. All three ate the meat in silence, but only small bits at the time. Then the person, who seemed to be the captain, looked up with fatty roasting oil in his long beard and nodded approvingly at the two others. They both nodded back with a smile, as if in agreement. All three headed for the salads, and one of the village women brought more meat. Gladys and Jenny watched the trio indulge themselves. They had never seen three small, stocky people eating so much and in such a voracious way. Food and roasting oil smeared the long beards of the two men. The woman, who wore a big white apron with colourful flowers, was cleaner but had roasting oil smeared all over her rosy cheeks.

Gladys and Jenny joined John and Neil, who were sitting on the ground, leaning against a pair of coconut palms.

'Did you see the three?' Gladys asked, and both Neil and John nodded.

'Interesting,' Neil said and looked across to the three crew members who were now into their fourth helping, served by one of the village women.

Behind John, Augustine appeared and sat down. John shook his hand and thanked him for the splendid meal, but Neil quickly asked, 'What kind of meat is the large leg?'

Augustine moved so he could look straight at all four cruisers and quietly murmured, 'Please do not tell.'

Then he changed to French and said, 'C'est de la viande de cheval — ils pensent que c'est de la chair humaine!'

Augustine looked at Gladys, who giggled with a big smile. She translated, 'He says, it is small horse leg, prepared so it looks like a human leg.'

Augustine continued, 'I had to kill our small horse, but I can easily buy four or more for the money paid.'

Black Pearls

Just west of the Manihi Atoll in the Tuamotus Archipelago, French Polynesia, is another atoll called the Ahe Atoll. In contrast to Manihi, which mostly adheres to the Mormon faith, Ahe has two churches, a Catholic and a Protestant. A visit to the only village, Tenukupara, which harbours about 100 people, reveals a dysfunctional society, judging by the many high stone walls with the dense mats of sharp glass on the top. In the Manihi village of Paeua which has about 400 inhabitants, there is nothing like that.

The only grocery shop on Ahe looks like a small fortress with walls around and with only a narrow entrance blocked by a free-standing inside wall. A visitor must turn left or right to get into the shop. The wall appears protecting the grocery shop from someone approaching armed on horseback.

John and Gladys arrived at the anchorage off Tenukupara in their 40-foot yacht "Sunset Dreaming" after sneaking through the narrow reef entrance on the incoming tide. It had been a short leisure cruise from Manihi just 8 nautical miles away. Getting through the reef entrance is the easy part. But reaching the anchorage is difficult because the charts or plotter does not show the many coral pillars, reaching up from the bottom to just below the surface of the lagoon, called "bommies".

Gladys was at the bow, holding on to the forestay, looking down in the water, directing John at the helm. Slowly they found their way through the bommie field. But there was another significant obstacle to avoid — the pearl oyster cultures. They were ropes, suspended between submerged buoys just below the surface. The only navigational aid was two red markers, indicating a no-anchor zone by the jetty, allowing a supply vessel to dock safely without interfering with visiting yachts. John and Gladys first thought that they were the only yacht in the atoll, but coming closer to the village, they spotted a large, thin white yacht on anchor. That did not bother them; they dropped the anchor some 300 meters away after checking the bottom for bommies and pearl cultures with their echo-sounder.

John turned the engine off and covered the mainsail. The couple settled down in the cockpit, enjoying biscuits and a cup of tea. Gladys was comfortable on the canvas pillows with her back resting against the cabin wall. As she always did, she started scanning the world around her with their marine binoculars. It had been Gladys' entertainment for some time. Every time they arrived at anchorages or in marinas, Gladys was watching every move with binoculars. She was given the nickname "The Harbourmaster" by her cruiser friends. When invited on board, they always asked, 'Hi Gladys what's new in the harbour?'

She knew the comings and goings, and the details of the yachts, even the specifics of the laundry hanging out to dry. She discussed her observations with her cruiser friends. After all, there was not much for her to do. John just laughed but asked her many times for bits of information he needed.

Gladys scanned the village and disappointingly declared, 'Not much in there!'

After looking at the coconut trees and Casuarina's on the reef fringe, she turned her attention to the other yacht.

'I think I have seen this one before; it's a MacGregor M65,' she said with the experienced voice of a seasoned yachtsman. 'I think we saw him in Banderas Bay before we left Mexico!'

'Can I have a look?' John asked, and she handed him the binoculars. 'Yes, you are right, he looks familiar. I think it is "Gigi". When I was in the regatta, everybody called him "the stick". I think he was in Hiva Oa when we checked in, but he left in a hurry. Remember when the supply vessel arrived? He was on the dock kissing a woman goodbye and embraced two more who came on the boat!'

'You are better at this than me,' Gladys exclaimed with a hint of jealousy in her voice.

John and Gladys arose at about eight and enjoyed a cockpit breakfast in the tropical morning sun. It was a splendid day. They jumped in their dinghy, which they had towed since they left Manihi, and motored into the harbour. It was comfortable and shallow in the inner harbour. They had no problem finding a rusty mooring ring where they could lock the dinghy with a marine steel wire. The couple walked with their light backpacks through the main street. There were only a few people around, and they quickly learned that the locals kept a safe distance, leaving them to their devices. They walked through the village and looked at the two churches and the broken glass-covered walls. Gladys said,

'This place looks a bit disappointing; don't you think?'

'Yea, you are right. Let's go to the grocery shop and see what information we can get.'

The grocer's name was Arri who introduced himself as the former mayor. Gladys browsed around in the shop while John was trying to get a conversation going — it was not easy. Gladys came to the counter with a load of biscuits and a few cans of exotic seafood. Dropping it on the counter, the grocer smiled. He calculated the cost and presented it to Gladys while chatting away about his family and the difficulty of living on a remote island.

He ignored John completely. Gladys had no problem involving herself in the conversation, and it did not take long before the grocer revealed the troubles of the atoll.

There was a state of war between the congregations of the two faiths. The grocer said that he left the honourable position as a mayor, like many before him, because of the religious resentments.

'Oh,' he said, 'it's the priests who are fueling the problem; they can never agree on anything.' John came in and asked, 'What's the problem?'

The grocer turned away from Gladys and towards John, looking a bit angry.

'The catholic priest will not give the youths any freedom, only condemnation. The protestant minister wants everybody to sit in the church for hours on end while he is gabbling away on the bible. The priests hate one another, driving a wedge between the two congregations.'

Gladys looked disturbed and held her hand across her mouth. She looked at John with a familiar look; it meant shut up!

'You see,' the grocer said, '"Thou shalt not steal", applies on this island only within congregations. The elderly lady next door came in this morning and told me that someone had entered her yard and stolen all her drying fish off the line!'

The grocer sat down on his stool with a sigh and looked at Gladys. She did not know what to say and asked a question which was a kind of diversion, or maybe not.

'Have you met the people on the long yacht out there?'

She looked in the direction of the anchorage.

'Yes,' the grocer said, 'the captain is a Catholic monk; he comes here regularly.'

John rolled his eyes and thought, 'Catholic monk, my ass.'

Gladys paid the bill and asked, 'Is there anybody on the atoll selling black pearls?'

The grocer looked at Gladys and John with a searching stare as if he was looking straight through them. John turned around, and to his astonishment, he saw the captain of Gigi standing in the doorway, dressed as a monk in the traditional black tunic with a scapular and a pointed hood. He had a well-groomed black beard.

'Well, who do we have here; isn't it the captain of Gigi?'

The friar looked displeased, and instead of greeting his fellow sailors, he turned towards the grocer and said, 'Can I please have the collection for the Archdiocese?'

The grocer produced a small leather bag with a seal and handed it to the begging friar. John looked surprised and said, 'Oh, you collect money while cruising Polynesia?'

The friar gave John a firm stare and replied somewhat angrily, 'I belong to the Order of Friars Minor, a Franciscan Order called the Capuchins. We do not own any wealth and are encouraged by the example set by Pope Francis in the call for truth and transparency in financial dealings in the church and human societies. It is my job to ensure the collect from the church for the Archdiocese is safely brought to Papeete.'

The captain friar turned around and disappeared out through the narrow gateway in the wall. The grocer sat on his stool, raised his shoulders and with a disapproving expression said, 'Here goes the Catholic congregation's monthly harvest of black pearls!'

Gladys and John brought their groceries back to the boat and settled in the cockpit, enjoying their lunch. Gladys took the binoculars from the teak box and looked at Gigi. After a long searching look, she quietly said, 'Tickle my toes, I believe two ladies are sunbathing on the foredeck. I don't think they have anything on!'

She handed the binoculars to John, who observed Gigi in silence. Gladys got impatient and said, 'Well, what do you see?'

'Yes, I think you are right, he answered, it's the life of a monk.'

He gave Gladys a mischievous smile and handed her the binoculars back. She looked again at Gigi, and with giggling laugh exclaimed, 'Give my knickers a twist; even the captain is naked!'

In the early afternoon, a panga left a wooden jetty at a waterfront house across the harbour and came alongside. It was a young man who offered black pearls for sale. Gladys and John were impressed with the size and quality of the pearls and bought a fine collection for only $200. The young man looked satisfied with the transaction, as were Gladys and John. They now had pearls as Gladys wished and gifts for all the girls in their family. Throughout the evening, they heard loud music and laughter from the house with the jetty, and occasionally people were singing. There was a party going on, and the waterfront porch was full of young people. At midnight, the loud music and the laughter faded away.

John and Gladys were having breakfast in the cockpit shortly after sunrise, enjoying the rising sun and the calm blue lagoon. Gladys noted that Gigi was gone.

'They must have left very early. I didn't hear any motor noise,' Gladys said, somewhat disappointed.

As they sat with their coffee mugs, a large supply vessel entered the lagoon with the incoming tide and set course for the village jetty. The grey painted ship quietly slipped through the field of bommies and moored at the jetty. As a forklift moved pallets loaded with goods out of the hull, four uniformed gendarmes came down the ladder in front of a few disembarking passengers. They disappeared up the main street. Among the passengers was a priest and an official-looking person with a black briefcase.

The two men waited on the dock. Gladys studied the spectacle with binoculars and reported to John at regular intervals what was happening. 'I think it's a Catholic priest judging by his uniform; I wonder what that is about?'

When the jetty was cleared of passengers and the final pallets loaded into the hull, the four gendarmes came back with another Catholic priest. The priest was handcuffed and protested loudly in French, but the gendarmes did not seem to take much notice and pushed him along.

The gendarmes and their prisoner stopped at the ladder where the official-looking person with the black briefcase was waiting. The newly arrived priest was standing behind him. The official person opened his briefcase and took out a sheet of paper and read loudly in French to the prisoner. He finished and took a step backwards. The gendarmes dragged their prisoner up the ladder and disappeared below. The official-looking person and the newly arrived priest hurried up the main street. Before long, the official-looking person came back to the vessel alone and got on board. Two navy sailors pulled in the ladder and the mooring ropes. The ship left the jetty towards the lagoon entrance.

'I think the Ahe Atoll has a new Catholic priest,' Gladys said with a bit of surprise in her voice.

John nodded in agreement and said, 'Maybe we should check with Arri, the grocer, to find out what is going on?'

Gladys nodded with a smile.

Later in the afternoon, the couple got in their dinghy and motored to the jetty. Gladys didn't want to buy anything but grabbed a few tins of fruit and brought them to the counter where Arri sat on his tabouret. She did not waste any time and asked, 'What was all the policing about?'

Arri looked at her with a half-hidden smile and shook his head.

'They arrested our priest for embezzlement of the church funds. It seems every month he sold half the collect of black pearls to the Franciscan friar and kept the money for himself. He claims the friar directed him to do so and the money he kept was for his church. It has been going on for a long time. He claims the other half of the pearls was sent to the Archdiocese in Papeete. The gendarmes are looking for the friar, but he left very early.'

Arri, the grocer, tipped back on his stool with a sigh and muttered, 'Now we have a new priest. I wonder how he will be?'

After a pause, Arri the grocer continued, 'I don't think they will arrest the friar because he just traded pearls to the benefit of the Capuchins Order.'

Gladys paid for the fruit tins and said with a sigh, 'I am sorry to hear this, but we hope everything will be all right.'

Arri, the grocer, looked at John and Gladys and said, 'Maybe, but look what you have done. Thanks to you, most of our youths had a party last night. They drank a lot after spending all the money on whisky. They don't work today because of the hangover.'

Gladys looked sternly at Arri the grocer and said abruptly, 'Well, we didn't sell any whisky; we bought pearls!'

Gladys turned around and marched out of the shop with John in tow.

Suwarrow Reef

Onboard their yacht "Sunset Dreaming," John read for his wife Gladys from the book "Sailing Routes of the World." He began, 'Yachts crossing the South Pacific from east to west; Suwarrow Reef is a convenient stop sailing from Bora Bora in French Polynesia to Samoa or Fiji. Yachts usually choose a northern route via Suwarrow to avoid what among sailors is known as "The Dangerous Middle" or the South Pacific Convergence Zone. It is where the equatorial easterly winds converge with or bump into the south-east trade winds; it's an area of unsettled weather not to underestimate.'

John looked at Gladys, who was absorbed in her fashion magazine, but answered, 'Sound good to me — we don't want bad weather!'

John continued, 'Leaving Bora Bora onboard a sailing yacht; it will take about a week to reach Suwarrow enjoying downwind cruising with the trades. Yachts will enter on the incoming tide via a narrow channel and anchor in a blue lagoon in the lee of Anchorage Island. Here visitors will be met by the wardens, who will ask the captain and the crew to come ashore to fill in the custom papers and pay a small fee.'

In the early afternoon, after a week of sailing across the open sea from Bora Bora, John and Gladys entered the Suwarrow Reef lagoon on their yacht, Sunset Dreaming. There were six sailing yachts on anchor, of which one was a sizeable US-flagged catamaran. The other boats had arrived earlier and were a familiar sight. John and Gladys recognised them from Mexico and their time in Tahiti, but the US-flagged catamaran was new to them.

They launched their dinghy and motored to the landing site on the shore and were greeted by the two wardens, James, and John. The two wardens lived in a house on concrete poles secured in a strong foundation to protect the building, and the wardens, in case of a cyclone storm surge. Below the house was a large table, benches, and chairs where James provided a briefing and an instruction which is a precondition for any yacht wishing to anchor in the atoll. John and Gladys sat with James at the table to complete the paperwork and pay the anchoring fee. They were not allowed on any other island than Anchorage Island and only within a set boundary where the houses were. Under no circumstances where they allowed to explore the reef or the islands unless under oversight by the wardens. These restrictions did not bother Gladys and John, because the purpose of the stay was entirely relaxation after a week on the open sea.

When everything was in order, Gladys and John signed the guest book and shook hands with both wardens. With the typical well-known hospitality of the Polynesian people, the couple were offered a refreshing fruit drink. Then James said, 'Tonight we are having a potluck here, and that will allow me the opportunity to tell you a bit about the history of the atoll. Be here about seven.'

Most of the crews were onshore, either playing volleyball or talking with one another or the wardens. Gladys immediately greeted the ones she knew, and everybody was chattering away in happiness as if they had just met long-lost friends. John had to pull Gladys away because they need to prepare a contribution to the Potluck supper. Gladys, of course, had already made up her mind what to bring and had asked John, the warden, for some coconut husk.

'Don't worry,' she said, 'I have already decided to make a coconut fish curry; it's easy.'

At seven, people began to gather at the warden's quarters and placed food in abundance on the large table under the warden's hut. James loaded the provision donations in a blue plastic drum, which he closed with a black lid. With a drink in their hand, people sat or stood around the table. It was a lovely, warm evening.

James began by introducing themselves.

'We are custom officers from the Cook Islands Park authorities. It's our job to ensure the integrity of the national park. We stay here between cyclone seasons, hoping to be picked up after six months' duty.'

A burst of nervous laughter broke out, but quickly died. James continued, 'The Suwarrow Reef is a coral atoll with 20 small islets. The count of islets may vary because storm surges created by cyclones may sweep the low-lying ones temporarily away. The atoll is a part of the Cook Islands and a National Park.'

James paused as if he wanted to ensure that everybody was listening.

He continued, 'Although Suwarrow is far away from everything, it has attracted the interest of many people. In 1890, Robert Louis Stevenson and his wife, Fanny, visited the island, describing it as the most romantic island in the world. It was not the inspiration of her famous husband's book "Treasure Island" which was published seven years earlier, but the atoll is an actual treasure island. In the mid-nineteen century, a ship from Tahiti arrived to carry out salvage work. By chance, the captain found an old iron chest buried in the sand on Anchorage Island. Inside were gold and silver coins at a value today of about US$5 million. Later, in 1876, a New Zealander, Henry Muir, discovered a box while watching a turtle laying eggs. It contained gold and silver jewellery and coins. According to the legend, he could not carry the treasure with him and therefore reburied it. Unfortunately, Mair was killed by natives in the New Hebrides in 1891. He left no written record of where the treasure was buried.'

James pointed at a painted bust and a stone with an inscription just outside. He continued, 'The most famous inhabitant was Tom Neal, a sailor, who lived on the island on and off for fifteen years until 1977 and wrote a book about his life here called, "An Island to Oneself". The stone and bust commemorate his life. It reads: "1952—77. Tom Neal lived his dream on this island." Bizarrely, the atoll is named after a famous Russian general, Alexandra Vasilievich Suvorov because a vessel bearing his name landed on 17 September 1814. At that time, the general had been dead for thirteen years.'

James raised his glass and said, 'Ladies and gentlemen, enjoy your evening.'

The company descended on the abundance of food but was distracted by the arrival of a large center console dinghy with a powerful outboard. It was the couple from the American catamaran; two relatively young people. The woman was attractive and beautifully dressed in an exotic beach-going dress, which left most of the male cruisers gaping. The man was tall and muscular, with light hair and a charming smile. It was clear he made an impression on the cruising ladies. An unease spread through the company of gathered cruisers, until Neil, a fellow American, said, 'Welcome, you just missed James's interesting account of the history of Suwarrow.'

James emerged from the periphery of the company and said, 'Allow me to introduce Khristina and Alex.'

The couple shook hands with all the cruisers who helped Khristina off-loading the food she brought along for the Potluck. Alex smiled and placed a large cooler full of wine and beer on the table.

'Just help yourself, with modesty,' he said.

It was the start of an unusual potluck, which quickly became a party to remember. Khristina flew like an exotic butterfly among the cruisers, entertaining everybody with a rarely seen charm. The cruising ladies flocked around her to hear what she had to say, and she made sure that everybody got a compliment, which was appreciated. Alex moved around as a seasoned diplomat, talking to everybody, discussing boats, navigation, and South Pacific sailing experiences. Neil, his fellow American, was somewhat reticent compared to the other cruisers, and suddenly asked, 'I have noted that you carry another flag than the stars and stripes which looks Russian with a crowned two-headed black eagle. What does it mean?'

Alex turned towards him with a big smile and laughed.

'It's a long story, but it's a company flag for the business I am running. I have a large herd of milk cows in Oregon. It's like a big factory consuming cow food and producing milk,' Alex said and paused, looking at Neil. He could see that Neil was not satisfied and continued, 'I have Russian ancestors from a long way back. They came to the US in the early nineteen century with the Russian-American Company trading furs in Alaska and along the entire California coast. Our flag was the flag for the RAC. The company went bust in the mid-nineteenth century, and I thought the flag could be useful for my milk company. We sell a lot of milk to the states of the former Soviet Union.'

Neil smiled and said, 'I know a bit about the company's history when I studied at the university, and it's interesting to hear someone carry on the traditions. I am sure you know the reef is named after the RAC's vessel "Suvorov" commanded by its famous navigator, Mikhail Lazarev?'

Alex looked somewhat puzzled, but quickly gained his posture with a smile. He was surprised that someone in the party had a historical knowledge of something which had largely been forgotten.

Khristina came along to Alex who said, 'Khristina, Neil here seems to know a lot about the history of the RAC.'

Khristina looked at Neil with a smile and a peal of charming laughter. Neil looked at her and seemed to be impressed by her charm. He asked, 'I suspect your name is spelt with Kh?'

'Oh,' Khristina said, 'so you are familiar with Russian names?'

'No, not really, but there were a lot of students of Russian heritage who studied at the Department of Economic History where I was.'

Khristina touched Neil's cheek with her hand and said, 'It is time for a drink. Do you mind fetching me a glass of Champagne before it's all gone?' Neil obeyed because Alex had turned his attention elsewhere.

John had been sitting on a bench, talking to John, the warden. He had not paid attention to what everybody else was doing. He looked for Gladys and saw her in a happy conversation with Khristina. It looked and sounded as if they had known each other for a long time.

'It's remarkable what a little Champagne can do,' he thought.

John looked at the table and realised that everybody had tucked into the food, but he managed to get some bread, fish curry and salad. While he was munching, he felt a tap on his shoulder.

'I haven't said hello to you,' said Alex.

John turned around and grabbed his hand.

'Fine yacht you have. Isn't it Sunset Dreaming?' Alex asked.

'Yes, that ours,' John answered, 'The name of the boat is a bit pretentious, but that's the name it had when we bought it; we haven't been able to agree on anything new.'

Alex laughed and said, 'Our Cat is called "Pied de Vache".'

John looked at Alex and said, 'How do you explain this?'

'Easy,' said Alex, 'Pied de Vache is French for cow foot. A cow is a pair-toed animal with two asymmetrical claws, and a Cat has two similar shaped hulls. We decided that the name had to be something to do with a cow — after all, we sell milk.'

It was late when the party broke up, but everybody enjoyed the potluck. James wished everyone a good night and Alex raised his voice, saying, 'Tomorrow night Khristina and I would like to invite you onboard Pied de Vache for appetisers and a social poker game — no big money, just fun!'

In the bright moonlight, the fleet of dinghies dispersed over the bay to the various boats on anchor.

Safely back on Sunset Dreaming, Gladys and John prepared for the night. John quickly headed for the bunk, but Gladys wanted to sit in the cockpit with a cup of tea before she turned in. She sat comfortably on the pillows and leaned back against the cockpit wall next to the hatch, looking through one of her fashion magazines in the light from a small lamp above her head. After half an hour or so, she noticed two dark kayaks silently paddling away from the anchorage in the direction of Turtle Island on the westerly side of the lagoon. After two hours, the two dark kayaks came back paddling in the direction of Pied de Vache.

The following day was a leisure day. Cruisers came to the warden's quarters where John the warden had organised a demonstration of coconut collecting, crushing, and shredding. Everybody had a try, but it was clear who were the experts. Afterwards, the cruisers enjoyed a lunch John and James had prepared with charcoal-grilled coral cod, rice, and fruit. After a rest in the shade of the palm trees, in the hammocks, or at a game of beach volleyball, James took the cruisers to the other side of the island where he had a plastic drum full of fish below a big sign nailed to a coconut palm with the painted text: "Danger, Sharks, No swimming". He threw a fish in the water and within seconds, it was boiling with reef sharks. He fed the sharks fish, much to the delight of the cruisers, while shouting, 'Don't swim here, please!'

At darkness, a fleet of dinghies sailed in succession to Pied de Vache where Khristina and Alex welcomed them. Inside the spacious cabin, the main table next to the pantry was loaded with all kinds of delicate appetisers of smoke meats, pate's, olives, smoked oysters, pickled miniature octopus and squids. At the end of the table were rows of wine bottles. The cruisers and John, the warden, were overwhelmed by the hospitality. Alex immediately declared, 'Cool white wine and Champagne is in the cooler under the bench. Just help yourself, in modesty.'

It seemed to be his standard phrase of hospitality, which most of the cruisers ignored. After an hour, another table was cleared and made ready for the poker game. John did not play poker, and Gladys enjoyed the company with two other lady cruisers while now and then watching the poker game, and especially how Khristina was doing.

'Look at Khristina; she is like a fish in water in this poker game. Mighty, she has already won twenty dollars!'

The evening flowed along, as did the wine and the appetisers. Next to midnight, Alex left the poker table and announced loudly, 'Ladies and Gentlemen, we have a long trip tomorrow because we are heading to American Samoa. I believe that a few of you will do the same. So, I have to say goodnight — one final drink, please!'

At that point, most had had enough after a full day on the beach and in the sun. The party broke up, and the dinghies headed back. Alex gave John, the warden, a lift to the shore.

For Gladys and John, it was a short sail to Sunset Dreaming anchored next to Pied de Vache. Just as the last night, John headed for the bunk while Gladys had a cup of tea in the cockpit. After half an hour, she again noticed two dark kayaks paddling quietly towards Turtle Island. Two hours later, they returned.

Next morning, John and Gladys checked out with James at the warden's quarters. Pied de Vache had already left. They discussed the weather report with James, who warned them they might face wind, overcast skies and rain when approaching American Samoa, but he claimed they would be all right. Then, to John's surprise, James asked him whether they had seen anybody out and about in kayaks during the night. John said that he had not seen any movements of any kind. Gladys and John sailed back to Sunset Dreaming and prepared for departure.

John asked, 'Gladys, what is all the stuff you have in the big black plastic bag in the shower?'

'It's all the moisturiser, shampoo, and conditioner bottles I want to get rid of in Pago Pago.' Gladys had to pack all her bottles of moisturisers, shampoo, and conditioners below the bench because John would not accept a bag floating around in the shower cubicle while they were sailing. After all, it would take six days before they arrive in Pago Pago. The couple hurried on because the tide was close to being slack. If they did not leave at once, they would probably have to wait for the next outgoing tide.

They raised the anchor and waved goodbye to the remaining yachts and James and John on the shore of Anchorage Island. As they approached the inlet, John could feel that the incoming tide had started to run. He increased the power of the engine to get out and set the mainsail and genoa in a 15-knot wind from the East. John set the course to 240 degrees and looked over his left shoulder because of a monotonous sound. He grabbed the binoculars, and in the distance, he saw a helicopter hovering over a large white yacht which looked like a catamaran. Gladys sat on her pillows at her usual place on the starboard side.

'Can I have the binoculars, please?'

John obeyed, grabbed the microphone of their VHF radio, and said, 'Suwarrow, Suwarrow this is Sunset Dreaming over.'

The answer came quickly without the formalities of changing channel away from 16.

'Don't worry. It's the navy boarding Pied de Vache for inspection — have a good trip.'

Gladys and John had a fantastic three days of sailing and quickly approached American Samoa, but on the fourth day, the wind died, and it became overcast. They motored all night. In the morning, the wind picked up from the south-west, and by the time they reached the eastern tip of the island, it was blowing 20 knots. Both Gladys and John worked hard on Sunset Dreaming with reefed sails tacking all day to reach the inlet at dusk. They both felt relieved as they motored through the well-marked entrance adjoining the large inner harbour.

The Pago Pago harbour is surrounded by hills, many of which are around 1000 feet high. In the dark, they could only see the hills from the light of a factory and a large fleet of fishing vessels moored at the docks on the central northern shore. There were well-lit houses around, so they had no problem going into the anchorage. They had hoisted the yellow flag and expected to hear from the customs in the morning, but to their surprise, a strong easterly wind came down from the hills, making waves and white horses. It was raining.

As John turned Sunset Dreaming west, he spotted a long concrete jetty going out in the harbour. He said to Gladys, 'I think the anchorage is a bit further in than the jetty, but I am worried because our pilot says that holding is not good.'

Without comment, Gladys grabbed the VHF microphone and said, 'Pie de Vache, Pied de Vache, Pied de Vache this is Sunset Dreaming, Sunset Dreaming over.'

A quick reply came, and they heard Khristina's voice, 'This is Pied de Vache go to Channel 67.'

Gladys changed the channel and heard Khristina say, 'The holding at the anchorage is terrible; we are moored to the jetty. We have behind us a line attached to a red buoy with flashing light. Pass the jetty slowly and motor up against the wind. Grab the red buoy and pull in the line; a rope will follow. Drop a stern anchor after to ensure the wind will not swing you back and forth. Attach yourself to the rope and straighten the boat up. Got it?'

Gladys answered, 'Roger, Roger, stay on the channel.'

Khristina answered, 'Will do!'

It did not take long before they spotted Pied de Vache in the lights on the jetty. Gladys took the wheel while John was getting a spare anchor ready, and he jumped forward with a boatman's hook to get the buoy and the line. As he pulled the line in, he looked at the catamaran and through the rain saw Khristina and Alex waving at them. Safely tugged in behind Pied de Vache and the jetty they went below to prepare their evening meal. Getting out of their weather gear, John looked at Gladys with admiration and said, 'Gosh, you girls are smart, and he gave her a kiss on the cheek.'

The morning light revealed the full size of the harbour and the surrounding high hills covered in green vegetation, with houses and villas on terraces.

'No wonder,' John said, 'that this harbour was so important in World War II. You can hide a whole flotilla of ships.'

John prepared himself to go ashore to see the customs and take a bus to Costco's outside town for shopping. That was why they had decided to go to Pago Pago and then Apia later. Gladys had already earlier declared that she has no desire to go ashore — she needed rest.

John came back loaded with provisions, which he handed up to Gladys in the cockpit.

'Glad I didn't go; there would not have been room for me in the dinghy,' she said with a smile.

John got up in the cockpit and stored some of his purchases below the bench.

'I see you got rid of all your bottles in the black bag.'

'Yes, Khristina came over and took them away.'

Gladys had prepared a late lunch for John, which he gratefully munched down. The couple settled on the pillows in the cockpit with a cup of coffee. John talked about how easy it was to check-in at the customs and how far Costco was out of town.

'By the way, he said, I saw a sign at McDonald's that they have free Wi-Fi; we may drop in later.'

Gladys nodded and at the same time handed him a large signet ring in gold, 'Have a look.'

John stared at the ring and surprised exclaimed, 'Where did you get that from?'

Gladys didn't answer but said, 'Look closely at the large jade centerpiece!'

'I will be dammed — what is that?' he said, looking shocked.

With excitement, Gladys said, 'If you look closely, you can see a carving of an Arabic knife; it's called a Jamb or Janbiya, and below is a name in Arabic. It is surrounded by garnets — isn't it pretty?'

John couldn't believe his eyes and said, 'Tell me more about it!'

Gladys took the ring back and held it in her hand, saying, 'It belonged to the slain Tartar Khan at the siege of Izmail in 1790; that's at the Black Sea in an area then called Bessarabia. If you are to believe Lord Byron's epic poem "Don Juan," which I do, a beautiful young Muslim girl arrived with Don Juan at the battle after escaping the Sultan of Constantinople; her name was Leila.'

Now John couldn't believe his ears.

Gladys placed her hand on John's arm and said quietly, 'Relax and lean back; there is more to come. I met Khristina in St. Petersburg when I was studying Russian language and culture at the university there. She was in the same group of Americans. She told me she descended from an Arabic girl, Leila, who met

Field Marshal Alexandra Suvorov at the siege of Izmail. Leila travelled with him to all his battles until he died ten years later. She had two children with him. Her family fled Russia to the US at the start of the revolution in 1917. They were close to the Tzar and had no choice.'

'After her university studies, Khristina met Alex, whose name is Alexandra Baranov. It's the same name as the first Chief Manager of the Russian-American Company from its start to 1818. Before Suvorov died, he had planned to retire from the military, and as a puppet, Baranov started the RAC on his behalf. The capital was a large gold deposit. Years after Suvorov died, Baranov was afraid that their reserve would be seized by the Imperial Russian Navy and organised an expedition using the company ship "Suvorov". The ship's Captain, Michail Lazarev, was ordered to bury the gold deposit on the Suwarrow Atoll, along with Suvorov's family jewellery. That was the year 1817. In 1818, the Imperial Russian Navy took over RAC and dismissed Alexander Baranov. The gold came from Suvorov's conquests and was not passed on to the Russian Empire, but grateful Royals gifted the jewellery.'

Gladys paused and took a sip of her coffee, which now was cold. John quickly said, 'Do you want me to make you another one?'

'No,' Gladys answered, 'I have more to tell.'

She handed John another ring she had in her pocket.

'This once belonged to Catherine the Great. It was gifted to Suvorov after he conquered the fort at Izmail. His victory was regarded as a major blow to the Ottoman Empire.'

John stared at a white gold ring with a large pink diamond in the center surrounded by blue sapphires and many smaller diamonds.

'The center one,' he said, 'must be more than five carats. I have never seen such a beautiful piece and look at the clarity of the center stone!'

'Khristina gave me both rings as a memento,' Gladys said quietly.

Twice John looked at the ring and then at Gladys and said, 'But this is worth a fortune, how?'

Gladys leaned back and looked up in the sky, sighed and said, 'What I tell you now must be between us. If you want me to continue, you must promise me to keep your mouth shut irrespective of whatever happens in life.'

'Is this about your so-called previous job?'

'Yes,' Gladys answered, 'Khristina and Alex approached us with a proposal to recover the boxes that Lazarev buried. They were primarily interested in getting hold of Suvorov's treasures which her family consider their inheritance. Remember, they fled Russia at the start of the revolution and came with nothing except the clothes they wore. The family carried with them Suvorov's papers with detailed information on what to find and where. But they never had the means to go and look for it. I became the manager of the project because I was their operator when Alex and Khristina spied for us in Russia.'

John swallowed a lump and said, 'I thought that you were a secretary; not an operative?'

'John, there are no secretaries in CIA; did you expect me to sit and knit all day?' Gladys said, with a taste of disappointment.

John looked at his wife and said, 'I am deeply sorry, I should never have questioned your ability. Please accept my apology.' Gladys sighed and continued, 'We brokered a deal after fighting off the greedy boys of the department. Khristina and Alex should go to the Suwarrow Reef and locate the position of the boxes, which the papers said were on Turtle Island. The sub people will recover the boxes, which are heavy, during the coming cyclone season when there are no wardens. They have some other installations here which need maintenance.'

Gladys paused and closed her eyes and said slowly, 'Remember, the Kiwi's keep a close eye on this place. What happens next will not be in my final report. After several visits to Turtle Island, Alex and Khristina located the stuff with metal detectors and dug up the smallest box containing the inheritance. They placed the jewellery in my shampoo bottles and handed it to me on their return. We are now on American soil, so I handed it back. Years of experience have taught me not to trust the department when it comes to family treasures. John leaned forward and kissed his wife on her lips and said,

'You are some smart cookies!'

Dead Reckoning in the Dangerous Middle

An unfading calm had descended over the Danish shipping company, J. L. Pedersen Shipping Ltd., who's staff, on a regular shift, would be involved in hectic trading at Lloyds in London. The owner of the company had departed Copenhagen Airport on his annual winter vacation, this time for the Pacific Island Kingdom of Tonga. The company had more than thirty cargo vessels sailing all over the world. It was the shipping officer's job to find cargo for them all and ensure the shipment could be picked up and delivered to its destination. This job is only for professionals because understanding shipping and having useful contacts with all kinds of shipping people around the world, is a necessity for a successful business.

The company had one supertanker on a five-year lease from a Japanese company. It was the youngest shipping officer's task to find a cargo for the tanker, which was not an easy job. It was only when his superior eventually allowed him to place bids below cost he was successful; crude oil from Port Lagos, Nigeria, to Corpus Christi, Texas. The young shipping officer's problems did not end there, because every attempt to contact a stevedore in Nigeria had failed. A more experienced colleague whispered in his ear that he would never get a response before he had deposited $50,000 in a Swiss bank account. With his hat in his hand, the young shipping officer approached his superior yet again, who quickly approved the deposit. Everybody else knew that such a transaction was typical when dealing with Nigeria. His superior handed him the Swiss account details.

With the boss on his way to Tonga, feet came upon the desks, but only for a while. From nine to five, the company owner's secretary, Lucy, a stout woman in her late fifties, ruled the floor in her boss's absence, but during the night, the shipping officers were on their own.

A week later, a steady stream of telegrams began to arrive instructing the Insurance Department to purchase a second-hand, two-hatch freighter. The Insurance Department's people were dump-founded. Why buy an old freighter? J. L. Pedersen Shipping had disposed of its fleet of two hatch freighters years ago. But faithful to their boss, they located the MV Simba, belonging to the Danish East-Asian Company, already on the slip for maintenance at a small shipyard in southern Denmark. They got it cheap.

On the owner, Knud Pedersen's recommendation, the Personnel Department located an officer crew of four, to be brought out of early retirement. After all, J. L. Pedersen Shipping employed ship officers and crews for life.

Before long, a telegram from the shipyard arrived at the office.

'What are we going to do with thirty Polynesian men, without clothes, who arrived here by air in the middle of the winter?'

With a series of telegrams going back and forth, sailor's clothing and wet weather gear in exceptionally large sizes were purchased and in haste trucked to the shipyard. The next request was for the insurance people to register the vessel under the Tonga flag on behalf of "Bounty Shipping Ltd., New Hebrides, Tonga Islands," a company listed on the Singapore stock exchange. But the final test was for the shipping people to find a cargo which would bring the vessel to the South Pacific. It did not take long. Within a week MV Simba departed for Falmouth to pick up a cargo of ammunition and explosives for Christchurch, New Zealand, to be sailed through the Suez Canal, a conflict war zone. The Personnel Department was only responsible for the attractive "dangerous goods" remuneration to be paid to their officers. J. L. Pedersen Shipping Ltd. was the only registered bidder for the cargo.

When MV Simba passed through Torres Strait and crossed the longitude 143 degrees east, north-east of Australia, the ship officially changed owners, giving J. L. Pedersen Shipping a small net profit of $500.000 US.

Gladys and John, who were cruising the Pacific in their 40-foot yacht, Sunset Dreaming, had not enjoyed American Samoa which they found unfriendly and with few attractive anchorages. Consistent bad weather had, of course, influenced their opinion of the islands, but they were ready to leave. They decided to island-hop through Tonga on their way to New Zealand, where Sunset Dreaming would stay for the southern winter while they returned to the US summer.

John had spent time planning their trip to Tonga. Gladys paid only little interest, but occasionally asked questions, or read over his shoulders to monitor progress, something that often annoyed John.

'Why don't you plan some of the trips?' he complained.

'No, you are so good at it — I will stuff it up.' Gladys replied, boosting his self-confidence a little.

They both left it to that.

After a while, John took the logbook and sat down in the cockpit where Gladys was relaxing, sitting with legs up on comfortable marine-blue pillows supported by cushions, reading old second-hand fashion and interior decorating magazines she had picked up in San Diego.

'I suggest the first leg to be from Pago Pago to New Potatoes; it's 209 nautical miles,' John declared.

'What are New Potatoes?' Gladys asked.

'It's an island about halfway to Neiafu. It is spelt Niuatoputapu, but in the Cruising Guide, they call it New Potatoes, it's easier.

From New Potatoes,' John continued, 'we will go to Neiafu about 180 nautical miles further south. It means that each trip should last two to three days, weather permitting'.

Gladys nodded approvingly.

'I have also checked the weather forecast and it's fine; south-easterlies five to ten knots for the next three days. We will be on a southerly course and laughing,' John declared with a pawky sense of achievement.

At sunrise, Sunset Dreaming, with John and Gladys onboard, left Pago Pago through the narrow harbour inlet and set sail for a southerly course, governed by the south-easterly wind. The sky was blue, and the feeling of being underway with all sails set made them joyful. The enclosed Pago Pago, with its high hills, had given them a claustrophobic feeling they now left behind.

Before MV Simba reached the 143 degrees east longitude, Captain Anders Rasmussen asked the "spark," Peter Hansen, to send an encrypted telegram to the head office where he expressed his concern over the integrity of their cargo when the vessel officially changed owner. He received a short response, "We have noted your concern."

MV Simba was an old vessel, but it was well maintained. The policy of J. L. Pedersen Shipping was to replace ships when they reached fourteen years of age. This policy was for tax purposes only because, after that time, the company would have written down the value. MV Simba was built at the B&W shipyard in Copenhagen, and since its launch, no equipment was replaced because it was of high quality. The previous owner, the Danish

East-Asian Company, had kept everything original, including radio and navigation equipment. The only modern equipment installed by J. L. Pedersen Shipping was a new radar, because otherwise the vessel could not be certified by the Danish maritime authority. Captain Rasmussen knew too well that when MV Simba crossed the 143 degrees east longitude, his ship may no longer be insured.

The owner of the shipping company, Knud Pedersen, knew what he was doing when he instructed his office to appoint the officer crew of his choice. Captain Rasmussen and the Chief Engineer, Kurt Jensen, both had more than forty years of experience. The second officer, Søren Hansen, was the youngest with thirty years of experience. The "spark" or "Gnisten," the radio-telegraphist, Peter Hansen, had been in the company for thirty-five years. They had been sailing on nearly all the vessels of the company. One thing they all had in common was the knowledge of the needs and workings of an old ship like MV Simba. They admired her not just for nostalgia, but because of her qualities.

Before MV Simba left Nakskov in southern Denmark for Falmouth, the chief engineer, Kurt Jensen, had requested a long list of special oils, grease, and fuel to be loaded onboard in Falmouth. As soon as MV Simba docked in Falmouth, the captain and the spark headed for the local marine shop and bought a modern GPS chart plotter with antenna, quality cables and navigational software, covering most of the world. The spark bought an Automatic Identification System (AIS) unit which he installed on the bridge, several handheld VHF radios and two waterproof handheld GPS units: one for the bridge and another for the lifeboat. The captain had ensured that all charts they needed were onboard and updated. Despite all the modern equipment, when sailing, Captain Rasmussen still enjoyed taking their latitude every midday using a sextant. The GPS reading was just for comparison. Before leaving, the spark had checked all the lifeboats and rafts to ensure that safety equipment and emergency provisions were current; a standard procedure for all the company ships before leaving the harbour.

The Polynesian crew quickly got the hang of calling the ship officers their Danish nicknames and the second officer, Søren Hansen's nickname was "Styrmand"; the man who steers the ship. The radio guy was "Gnisten" in Danish or "the spark" in English. The chief engineer was called "Mester" or "Master" in English. In Danish, he was "maskinmester" hence the shortening "mester". Captain Rasmussen was referred to as "Kaptajn" or "Skipper," in English, Captain.

When John and Gladys reached New Potatoes, Niuatoputapu, in the northern reaches of Tonga, they were exhausted. The initial weather forecast looked like it would be a close reach, but it lasted only 18 hours. They could see the bad weather coming, and John said in a melancholic voice, 'I think King Neptune has deceived us; we just crossed into the South Pacific Convergence Zone. I had the feeling the SPCZ in these waters was nearby; it's not for nothing the area is called the "Dangerous Middle"!'

The weather got squally, and the wind changed from anything between 0 to 35 knots from all possible directions, even right on their nose. Gladys and John battled with the weather through day and night but eventually reached New Potatoes. They were lucky, arriving at midday and had good visibility. The weather had cleared, and they quickly found the passage through the reef; even when their GPS chart plotter did not show the reality. John knew that this can always happen because large areas have not been "ground truthed" with the electronic maps in their plotter.

The tide was not running, and they easily spotted and aligned the white triangles marking the navigational channel, due south.

'Remember what the pilot says, John, do not cut any corners, I will tell you when to turn southeast,' Gladys said while John focused on the chart plotter in front of him where their GPS position in the electronic chart was wrong.

When they got closer to a yellow marker, Gladys could see the reef marker near the anchorage described in their pilot.

'Turn now; southeast!' Gladys said firmly.

Slowly, Sunset Dreaming motored on, and after they had passed the jetty at Falehau village, they anchored in the bay on sand in 10 meters of water. The couple settled down in the cockpit with a cup of coffee and enjoyed the eye-catching view of the steep tree-covered volcanic cone of Tafahi, reaching more than 600 meters skyward. There was another yacht anchored further away.

MV Simba kept a steady 12 knots southeast along the Australian coast, well east of the Great Barrier Reef. They had side winds most of the time, but nothing which made captain Rasmussen change course. About 400 nautical miles north-west of New Zealand, they received a telegram from Bounty Shipping instructing captain Rasmussen to enter Cook Strait and dock in Wellington. He was also required to take on board a pilot. Captain Rasmussen duly reported the change in instruction to J. L. Pedersen Shipping in Copenhagen. The response was, 'We have noted your concern.'

When not busy in the engine room, Mester visited the bridge to discuss their progress, but as they approached New Zealand, the talk was about the changed instruction. Captain Rasmussen could see that Styrmand was worried. He shared his worries with Mester, whom he had known for many years. Gnisten joined in, and they were contemplating what precaution they could take. When they loaded the cargo onboard in Falmouth, both Styrmand and Gnisten had carefully checked what was loaded on board and that it was in accordance with the cargo manifest. They complained to the captain that the manifest was not specific, listing all boxes as "ammunition". Their concern subsided somewhat when they realised the receiver of the goods was the New Zealand Defense Force.

When MV Simba approached Cook Strait, they received a call

from the pilot on Channel 16; he was on his way to meet them. Two hours later, MV Simba was safely brought into Wellington Harbour and docked at Queens Wharf.

Captain Rasmussen looked at the wharf, shook his head, and said, 'We are not going to off-load our cargo here; it's for tourist ships!'

An hour later, two well-dressed heavy Polynesian men arrived in a taxi. They walked up the gangway, leaving their luggage on the dock. On the deck, captain Rasmussen and Styrmand, Søren Hansen, greeted the two Polynesian men. MV Simba's Polynesian crew, of which a few were watching the waterfront from the deck, recognised the two men, and were waving and cheering. The two Polynesian men waved back but were shown into the mess-room where they were offered a coffee or a Danish beer. They sat down with the two ship officers.

The two Polynesian men presented themselves as representatives of Bounty Shipping Ltd from Tonga. They informed the officers that the company had ordered bunkers, and that a harbour tanker would come alongside as soon as possible to commence fuelling. The two men inquired about the ship's provisions, but captain Rasmussen assured them they had enough to reach Christchurch. One of the two Polynesian men, who appeared to be the most senior, explained that MV Simba was not going to Christchurch, and gave the captain a written, signed instruction ordering him to take the ship towards Tonga, awaiting further orders. The senior Tonga man suggested to the captain that it would be best if he took additional provisions on board, so the ship's stores were full before departure. He informed captain Rasmussen that they were going with MV Simba on its journey north.

Captain Rasmussen asked Styrmand to get onto the bridge, inform Mester to prepare for taking onboard bunkers, and ask the cook for a list of what he needs. Captain Rasmussen added, 'There is a book in my cabin with a list of Wellington shipping suppliers. Let's get moving, and by the way, ask the crew to pick up the luggage of the two gentlemen left on the wharf.'

The captain installed the two Tongan men in the last available cabin and joined Styrmand on the bridge. Mester was there too. He was covered in dirt and oil and swearing over the sudden decision to bunker,

'What the devil is this? he complained.

We need to clean one of the starboard fuel tanks before we can refill it. I had to pump the sludge into drums, and the pump was leaking. I sincerely hope we can off-load the drums; otherwise, we will be short of space in the engine room.'

Styrmand asked Mester to calm down, assuring him that there was plenty of room available in the after-cargo hold. Mester Jensen left, pouting, for his oily world below.

Before long, a small harbour tanker came along, initiating a flurry of activity on deck. Less than two hours later, a large truck from a Wellington shipping supply company arrived, off-loading pallets of boxes with provisions carefully tallied by MV Simba's Polynesian purser before the ship's crane lifted it on deck. At dusk, MV Simba left Wellington Harbour and Cook Strait on a north-easterly course along the Kermadec Ridge towards Tonga, about 1300 nautical miles away. Captain Rasmussen handed Gnisten an encoded telegram to J. L. Pedersen Shipping, Copenhagen. An hour later, captain Rasmussen received a telegram: 'We have noted your concern. Lloyds in London is informed. Await instructions. For your eyes only.'

The 42-foot Beneteau, Déjà vu, with three men on board, the procurator for a crime syndicate and his two assistants, Milan Svoboda, a Slovakian, and Jim Baltzer, an American, had left Guayaquil, Ecuador. The assistants were men in their late twenties, having lived most of their adult lives undertaking petty crimes and spending time behind bars. It was in prison they met.

After release, they had worked themselves up in crime as drug dealers, in particular cocaine. They had learned their trade while in prison, and over time refined their skills, being cautious with an inconspicuous behaviour and appearance. They met their teacher in crime in prison and developed a trust which became useful when they were all released. Their teacher provided pre-packed cocaine, ensuring that their operation was covert. Only small amounts were delivered at any one time. Jim and Milan understood being caught with cocaine on them meant prison time. With their teacher's help, they developed an ingenious gadget, so from their long-legged pants could dispose of their stock of small bags of cocaine when they raised their hands. Soon the business was flourishing beyond their expectation.

One day, their teacher did not turn up. They searched for him in vain. They carefully observed his home for days, but no one came and went. They decided to enter his house to investigate, and here they found their teacher, tied up to a chair and shot with a single bullet through the head. They fled.

The two young men had no option but to try to find a new supplier. It was not without risks. Gangs operated within certain boundaries, and they soon realised that there were new people on what they had considered their turf. Little did they know that it was their teacher who had defended the area with a large group of associates, of which they were only a small piece of the puzzle. A lot of people they used to meet on the streets had disappeared, and their customers were too afraid to buy cocaine from them. It did not take long before they were picked up by the takeover gang and dragged bleeding in front of the new "Godfather" who was less appreciative of human lives. The two young men had to start over again, and hope to gain the confidence of their new boss who had absolutely no faith in them. Their earlier peaceful lives were turned upside down. Now they were no longer cocaine dealers on the streets, but a part of a larger organisation which demanded loyalty to the limit of self-sacrifice. Milan and Jim became apprentices in a murder squad, providing bodyguard services to the top people of the gang, including assassinations on request.

After two years of services, the two men were called to face their godfather. He recognised their services as satisfactory and gave them an assignment overseas. They were to accompany one of his procurators, as he called the people he trusted with purchases. Milan and Jim were to travel to Ecuador, where the procurator was going to buy a large quantity of cocaine. The cocaine was to be loaded into a yacht purchased for the purpose, a 42-foot Beneteau. They were to assist the procurator, as he required, and join him in bringing the cargo safely across the South Pacific to Australia.

Milan and Jim had never been at sea or overseas before. Equipped with false passports, they and the procurator crossed the Mexican border and flew from Mexico City to Quito. From there, they travelled to the Guayaquil Yacht Club in Puerto Azul on the outskirts of Guayaquil. They located the 42 foot Beneteau, Déjà vu, which the procurator had bought from a yacht broker over the internet, and paid a deposit. The broker had loaded the yacht with 250 kilograms of cocaine and supplied two M16 assault rifles and three Colt handguns with the necessary ammunition. The broker had also equipped Déjà vu with provisions enough for three men for two months. The broker was familiar with this type of transaction, and for the procurator, it was his third trip from Ecuador to Australia. As soon as the procurator accepted the yacht, he organised transfer of the purchase price to an account of the broker's choice. The next day at sunrise, Déjà vu sailed out of the river and began a Trans-Pacific crossing. They were lucky with the weather. After 45 days at sea, they passed north of Pitcairn Island and into French Polynesia, logging a distance of 4275 nautical miles.

It was not an easy voyage for Milan and Jim, who had no sailing experience. The procurator assisted with the initial introduction of the boat. He then set the course and left it to Milan and Jim to sail the yacht. Every morning after the procurator had sobered up, he checked their position, plotted their position on a chart, and gave new instructions. He spent his time between meals on his bunk and emerged before sunset, claiming his five o'clock drinks. After five hours, he found his bunk, drunk. He had ensured that the booze and the guns on the yacht were locked up, and in threatening terms discouraged Milan and Jim from even considering an attempt to help themselves.

As they entered the Tuamotus, the procurator became more alert, and ensured that the boys steered well clear of all the reefs and atolls. Without clearing customs, they anchored at Papeete with a French flag flying from a flagpole after. Leaving Milan and Jim on the boat, the procurator made a quick excursion to a supermarket and returned by taxi with a load of provision and booze. As soon as the provisions were loaded on board, Déjà vu left Papeete for Tonga, 1462 nautical miles away.

Déjà vu progressed well on an easterly course despite the ever-changing weather conditions. Both Milan and Jim felt more confident as they learned how to sail the yacht. But the navigation was the procurator's domain, and he did not attempt to involve his two crew. The procurator received a call over his satellite phone and started to search the yacht while swearing. He looked through every locker, every storage compartment, searched under benches and throughout the engine room. Then he turned his attention to the cockpit. He opened the hatches and with a torch searched every space. He had to bend his body down into the hatches to search the space between the hull and the inner glass fiber wall. With a cry, he wriggled himself out of the starboard hatch with a small black box in his hand. The box had a short antenna.

'Look, he said with a sort of triumph in his voice — we have been tracked!'

Milan and Jim looked at the box while the procurator explained that the gadget, he had located, had sent regular signals to a satellite above, reporting their position to someone, possibly the DEA, the Drug Enforcement Agency. In a rage, he threw the box overboard and immediately attended to his chart and gave instruction to change the course. Déjà vu headed north-east towards the northern Tongan Island, Niuatoputapu or New Potatoes.

Just after sunrise, Gladys parked herself in her favourite position in the cockpit, enjoying a morning cup of coffee while looking over the village and the towering volcanic cone, Tafahi. John came up with his coffee and placed himself on the other bench, accepting the fact that all the pillows were already in use. He settled himself on the bench cushion, leaning against the coaming. Gladys was scanning her surroundings with their marine binoculars and checked the neighbouring yacht, a bit deeper in the bay.

'John,' she said, 'I think it's a 42-foot Beneteau. When it swung around, I had a glimpse of the name; I think it's called Déjà vu, but I do not know the nationality. Judging from the flag, it could be Dutch or French.'

John munched on a muffin and nodded, giving the impression that he was interested, which he was not. Gladys continued, 'I can't see anyone on board. I suggest we take a stroll by when we go ashore to explore the village.'

John was leaning back, looking up at the drifting clouds with half-closed eyes still munching on his muffin.

'John,' Gladys said with a firm, irritated voice, 'are you listening?'

John looked at Gladys. 'Yes, I'm listening; what did you say?'

Gladys shook her head and repeated her suggestion. 'I suggest we take a stroll to the boat over there when we go ashore.'

'That's fine with me,' John said while taking a slurp of his coffee mug.

An hour later, John got their dinghy in the water and secured the outboard on the stern plate. 'Look at the water; it is crystal clear — isn't it nice?' John said, giving Gladys a helping hand so she could get into the dinghy.

In bright sunlight, they slowly motored across the blue lagoon, admiring the lush green backdrop of the volcano cone. They came alongside the 42-foot Beneteau, but there was no-one on the deck. John ran the dinghy to the after platform so they could look into the cockpit. An unshaven, tired-looking younger man peered out from the cabin.

'Sorry if we woke you up, but we just wanted to say hello. We anchored last night,' John said, and pointed towards Sunset Dreaming.

The unshaven man got further up and into the cockpit. He wore a pair of dirty shorts and a t-shirt, which had seen better days.

'Hello,' he said and lifted his hand.

'Are you staying here for long?' John asked.

The response was short and in an undefined dialect. 'No, we are soon leaving.'

'Oh good, we wish you a safe journey. Maybe we will meet again.'

John sat down on the transom, let the 42-foot Beneteau go, and motored towards the village jetty.

'Gosh,' Gladys said with a touch of resentment, 'did you see how dirty the cockpit was, and there were empty beer bottles everywhere? I wonder how this boat would look like inside?'

She turned around on her seat, looked towards the village and the lush green backdrop, away from the 42-foot Beneteau.

The following morning early, Sunset Dreaming with John and Gladys onboard left New Potatoes, or Niuatoputapu, heading south towards Vava'u some 180 nautical miles south. The 42-foot Beneteau, Déjà vu, had left in the middle of the night.

The unsettled weather of the SPCZ had metamorphosed into splendid sailing weather with blue sky and a steady 15-knot easterly wind. Sunset Dreaming was running eight to ten knots parallel to the waves, making it fast, enjoyable sailing. After sunset, the wind dropped a little but kept a steady 10 knots. At midday on the second day of sailing, Gladys and John had the Vava'u Island group in sight. In the early afternoon, they entered the "Neiafu fjord," one of the most beautiful natural harbours in the Pacific. They found their way into Neiafu and tied up to an available buoy at "The Mooring Base," just south of the township. It was not their intention to stay there for long, but they had to check in with the Tonga customs and immigration people.

After a good night's sleep, John and Gladys motored their dinghy to the foreshore. John had only one thing on his mind; to get a cold glass of draft beer at the Mango bar. Neither he nor Gladys had been to Tonga before, but they had heard about "The Mango". It was a place where cruisers from all over the world met when sailing in the Kingdom of Tonga; they were both looking forward to it. Gladys was not that eager, though; after all, it was still morning, and she expected that beer was something cultivated people first consumed after five pm.

'John,' Gladys said with unwavering determination, 'first we will go to the customs and immigration to get our papers in order. Then we can take a stroll through the town. I will buy you lunch.'

John gave Gladys a disappointed look but accepted his fate. After securing their dinghy, Gladys took John's hand and together they walked along the waterfront to the custom and immigration house not far away.

The couple enjoyed the township and its friendly people. They visited shops and a market, realising that people were genuinely welcoming. Gladys could not help herself and shopped for all kinds of souvenirs, scarfs, and sarongs. Occasionally, Gladys fancied a t-shirt for John as a subconscious bribe, making him an unaware accomplice in her shopping indulgence. John was not interested in adding more t-shirts to the substantial collection he already had on board, but that did not discourage Gladys. She managed to persuade him to accept a Tongan male necklace, which she had seen on the Tonga men she eyed.

'It's a love present from your wife,' was her convincing argument.

'You will love wearing it; it makes you look young and beachy,' Gladys insisted while securing the necklace around his neck, lightly pinching his cheek, and presenting a smile John knew too well. He was speechless.

At half-past four, John had the sign in sight he had been longing for: The Mango Bar. Unintentionally, Gladys slowed her stride, but John was like a milkman's horse spotting the home barn. No amount of bridle could curb his determination. Short of breath, the couple sat down in the comfortable bamboo lounge chairs under the long marquee, facing the waterfront and all the yachts on their moorings. John only needed to give the waiter a look, and two fingers before two cold pints of beer emerged, accompanied by a smile and a, 'Welcome to the Mango!'

Cruisers crowded the bar, mixed with a couple of locals, occupying nearly all the bamboo chairs. Chatter and laughter filled the air. It did not take long before a couple of fellow cruisers appeared at their table. Gladys and John recognised them from back in Mexico. More cruisers arrived, greeting one another as long-lost friends. Pints came and went. It was smiles all around. John found himself hanging on to the bar talking to a few cruisers, while Gladys sat comfortably in a bamboo lounge chair, chatting with a couple of cruising ladies. John enquired carefully about the 42-foot Beneteau, Déjà vu. 'Does anybody know that boat? Has it been here to check in?' John told his cruiser friends about the encounter, and the appearance of the boat, disguising his inquisitive interest as just casual.

At 7 p.m., Gladys and John joined a few cruiser friends for dinner at a local restaurant across from the Mango. John had to visit the men's room several times to get rid of the draft beer, which seemed to fill up his bladder as soon as it was empty. Gladys looked at John every time he left and asked, 'Are you going again?'

The other cruisers laughed, but someone came to John's rescue.

'When a man has to go, he has to go!'

Two hours later, John and Gladys again found themselves in the Mango, but an hour after they escaped and motored back to Sunset Dreaming, where Gladys happily off-loaded her purchases below. Exhausted, John stayed in the cockpit, making himself comfortable on the cushions and the pillows. After a while, Gladys appeared with two mugs of coffee and reclaimed a couple of pillows which she considered hers.

'Did you get any information about Déjà vu?' Gladys asked.

'Nah, nobody seemed to know anything, or maybe they don't want to tell,' John uttered with a resigned sigh.

'Well,' Gladys said, 'the yacht was sold in Ecuador to three men, two Americans and one Slovakian. They left Guayaquil Yacht Club in Puerto Azul two months ago and headed straight to Tahiti and then to Tonga. They are expected to go to Australia from here.'

Surprised, John sat upright against the coaming.

'Where did you get all that information from?' he asked.

'There was an SMS from the office on the SAT phone. They have a tracker on the boat. It's loaded with cocaine,' Gladys answered casually.

'I thought you had retired,' John said.

'I have, but the office thinks I have not.'

'Why is that?' John asked, a bit unsatisfied.

'Cause we are here,' Gladys answered unwillingly. 'And by the way, there is a two-hatch freighter coming our way loaded with ammunition and explosives. It was supposed to off-load the cargo in Christchurch, but the vessels new owners redirected the ship to go north towards Tonga. Nobody knows why. I think this is going to be fun.'

With a deep sigh, John leaned back, covering his eyes with both hands.

The owner of J. L. Pedersen Shipping, Knud Pedersen, was furious when he received the information that MV Simba had not arrived in Christchurch, but instead was diverted to Tonga. His company was a highly respected family-owned shipping company, established in the 1880s, and from a modest beginning developed into a modern shipping company with numerous subsidiaries. The company operated a fleet of so-called reefer-vessels, vessels with refrigerating capacity, carrying fruit and vegetables all over the world. Above all, the company was not all about money, but was active in education and various charities related to shipping and industry development. The family always required their children, when entering the company, to be honest in their business dealings, and committed to leave a legacy of achievement in the society, at home and abroad. To be frank and open in their business dealings was of utmost importance. The thought that J. L. Pedersen Shipping was an accessory to cargo theft would be detrimental to the company's reputation.

When arriving in Tonga, the Danish Consul had informed the King, Tāufaʻāhau Tupou IV, about Knud Pedersen's arrival, primarily because he hoped it would improve his standing at the court. The king and his government had made some problematic economic decisions, wasting millions of dollars, forcing the government to take various actions to improve the nation's bottom line. Among them, the establishment of a shipping register and the company, Bounty Shipping Ltd. The king had done a lot to improve the welfare of his people. With his increasing age, his children had gained excess influence, not always in the interest of the Tonga nation, but rather to avariciously grow their Swiss bank accounts.

The purpose of Knud Pedersen's vacation in Tonga was to escape the Danish winter, to spend time with his wife, enjoying the white sandy beaches, the coconut trees and the blue sea. He had rented a beachfront villa where he expected to relax and prepare himself for the working year ahead. The couple had planned the trip for some time. Now he found himself with a problem by accepting an invitation to meet the king because he wanted to get an overzealous consul off his back.

The king had received Kurt Pedersen and his wife, Caroline, with great hospitality and a lavish banquet. They had to shake hands with an endless lineup of officials, and finally, his daughter, Princess Royal and son, the Crown Prince. Little did Knud know what the two siblings were cooking up behind the scenes. He had heard rumours about their lavish lifestyles, and that they had employed a financial adviser as an official "court jester"! But after the official protocol was over, the King, Kurt and Caroline sat on a large veranda in comfortable bamboo armchairs overlooking the blue sea. A cool soft breeze aired the patio. The king talked passionately about his people and the history of the kingdom. He mentioned that his biggest problem was to find employment for young men, and the need to improve the exchange of goods and services between the many islands. The king told Kurt about the establishment of Bounty Shipping Ltd, but that there was no one with experience in shipping in Tonga. Kurt boldly suggested to the king that he knew about an old but good quality two-hatch freighter which might suit his needs as a supply vessel operating within Tonga, and further away, if an opportunity came along. Kurt ensured he would be able to find a cargo which would bring the ship to Tonga and reduce the purchase price considerably. The next day, mediated by the consul, an agreement was reached. Proceeds from the Tongan shipping register would cover the cost of the vessel, and J. L. Pedersen Shipping would transfer the proceeds of the freight to Bounty Shipping. He would also provide ship's officers to bring the ship to Tonga, while Tonga would provide thirty non-commissioned sailors. A "fee for service" of USD 500,000 would be paid to J. L. Pedersen Shipping before the vessel officially changed owner. During an elaborate ceremony, a memorandum of understanding was signed, and Kurt Pedersen forwarded his instructions to the company Insurance Department, leaving them to deal with the legal aspects of the contract.

After getting the unwelcoming news about MV Simba's diversion to Tonga, Kurt Pedersen got into action. He quickly instructed his Copenhagen office to inform the owner of the cargo, the New Zealand Defense Force, and Lloyds of London as the insurer, that Bounty Shipping Ltd. had taken control of the cargo and thereby forfeited their contractual commitments to J. L. Pedersen Shipping. Now Kurt's concern was his officers onboard MV Simba.

MV Simba tugged her way north at a steady pace along the Kermadec Ridge. They passed Raul Island on the starboard side. The weather was acceptable in captain Rasmussen's view, but the two representatives for Bounty Shipping spent all their time on their bunks. The crew was engaged in maintenance work under the supervision of Styrmand Hansen. There was always a Polynesian crew member at the wheel, 24 hours a day.

Both Captain Rasmussen and Styrmand Hansen had noted that a grey prop plane had been following them north, appearing now and then at a height where identification was not possible. Captain Rasmussen was in no doubt that it was the New Zealand Airforce. The two Polynesian men from Bounty Shipping appeared on the deck, where one of them was having a lengthy conversation over a satellite phone. When MV Simba was about 200 nautical miles from Tongatapu Island, the largest island in Tonga, and home to the capital, Nuku'alofa, the two men from Bounty Shipping appeared on the bridge, armed. They handcuffed the captain and Gnisten. When Styrmand Hansen appeared, he got the same treatment. They forced captain Rasmussen to call Mester up on the bridge. The men tried to handcuff Mester, but he did not give up that easily. He fought back and was dealt a blow to his head. Unconscious, he was handcuffed.

The two Polynesian men ordered the captain to stop the vessel, which he did. Then they commanded the crew to launch one of the lifeboats and ordered the ship officers onboard. Two Polynesian crew assisted the handcuffed officers down the ladder to the lifeboat. When all four were in the lifeboat, one of the Polynesian men from Bounty Shipping, who appeared to be the leader, dropped the key to the handcuffs down in the lifeboat, released the mooring and waved them goodbye with a smile. MV Simba steamed away towards Tongatapu, leaving the lifeboat and the four officers to their own devices.

The officers got the oars out and started to row. Mester was not well, so he had to lie down in the bottom of the boat resting on a couple of life jackets. Gnisten opened the locker aft, and in triumph pulled out one of the handheld GPSs he had bought in Falmouth. He also reported to Captain Rasmussen that he had replaced all the emergency provisions onboard before they left Falmouth. In the baking sun, they rowed north, hoping to reach one of the Tonga Islands. They all knew too well that their real enemy was the shortage of fresh water, but for now, there was enough onboard.

As MV Simba sailed north, the New Zealand recognisance plane flew low over, which made the two men from Bounty Shipping nervous. They had been told that in Tonga territorial waters there was nothing the Kiwis could do. Little did they know about the diplomatic row which had erupted between New Zealand, the UK High Commission, and the Kingdom of Tonga. Nobody in the government in Nuku'alofa knew about the cargo that MV Simba carried, only that they had bought a two-hatch freighter to service their many islands. The government acted on principles and rejected the New Zealand request to board the vessel. MV Simba had instructions to go directly to the northern island of Vava'u, to dock at Neiafu and take on a cargo destined for the provisional Government of Bougainville, Papua New Guinea.

As MV Simba had Tongatapu to starboard, the Bounty Shipping satellite phone rang. The two men from Bounty Shipping were ordered to leave the vessel and board a speedboat, which was on its way. Bounty Shipping feared the New Zealand Navy would board MV Simba because a patrol vessel had left Niue heading towards Tonga. Off Pangai in the Ha'apai group, midway between Tongatapu and Vava'u, the New Zealand Navy boarded MV Simba under Admiralty Law, declaring MV Simba a vessel subjected to piracy. An agreement between the Kingdom of Tonga and New Zealand allowed MV Simba to be escorted to Tongatapu with a New Zealand officer crew. A Tongan court established the New Zealand Armed Forces as the rightful owners of the cargo. A warrant for the arrest of the two representatives of Bounty Shipping of unknown identity was issued, but no-one was ever caught.

The lifeboat with the four J. L. Petersen Shipping officers was drifting north towards Fiji and further away from Tongatapu. After a week, they were well northeast of Tongatapu when the weather changed. They had given up rowing because it made no difference to their speed and direction over ground, Captain Rasmussen had declared. Every day at midday, Gnisten had placed a waypoint in his handheld GPS, noted their position and shut it down to save the battery. Captain Rasmussen had a small notebook with him, and he and Styrmand drew up a grid of longitude and latitudes where they plotted their position. By timing a small piece of paper tossed overboard from the bow to the stern, they estimated their speed through the water. Although captain Rasmussen recognised the accuracy of Gnisten's GPS, he still followed his old ways of dead reckoning. Nobody argued with him because they all knew that he was a capable seaman, GPS or not.

The change in weather and strong winds forced the lifeboat eastwards, and to their relief, low coral islands appeared on the horizon. Gnisten declared they were entering a large string of coral reefs with a few small islands, and maybe they would be protected because they were approaching from the lee. Under Captain Rasmussen's recommendations, they took to the oars and headed for the closest island they spotted. Gnisten declared the island had no name. They knew too well that the island was no rescue, but possibly a trap, if they didn't find freshwater.

Déjà vu stayed only one day in Niuatoputapu before heading south. The procurator was nervous and did not know what strategy to adopt. His first thought was to sail away from their planned route, but then changed his mind. Now he wanted to go south and find an isolated atoll where they could stay for a while. Milan and Jim noticed he drank far more than previously, and spent most of the time sleeping on his bunk, if not drinking. Déjà vu passed Vava'u well east of any of the islands to avoid observation. With the sight of any sail or vessel on the horizon, Milan and Jim were ordered to change course and avoid any close encounter.

Just south of Vava'u, the weather changed, and so did the wind. Large cumulus clouds were building up, and there was lightning everywhere. They observed rain clouds all around them and the wind became unpredictable, going from barely a puff to gale force within minutes. Jim tried to wake up the procurator, but he was too drunk. Suddenly, they found themselves in a lightning storm. The rain poured down and the strong wind forced them to run downwind with only a reefed genoa set. The waves and wind lifted their wide stern and the skeg rudder, making it difficult to steer. Déjà vu skated from side to side; the two helmsmen had no choice but to hang on. With a massive noise and force, lightning hit the mast and ran down the shrouds and mast, leaving a burned smell. Milan got an electric shock from the steel wheel and fell backwards into the well. He and Jim regained control, but Déjà vu was still swaying from side to side as they ran downwind. They realised that the lightning had caused a large rift in the genoa. At one stage, the wind dropped so much they could assess the damage. The lightning had destroyed their chart plotter, the radar, and the radio equipment. The only equipment which appeared to work was the log instrument. It showed the boat's speed and distance travelled through the water. They had no idea where they were heading, except that the compass pointed due west. It did not occur to them that the only navigational option was dead reckoning by plotting the course and the distance travelled on a chart. Drift by wind and currents was the black joker in the game.

The strong easterly wind continued. Milan and Jim tried to change course towards the south as the procurator instructed, but every time they turned the yacht, the rift in the genoa got longer and eventually shredded the entire sail. It was now useless. They tried to hoist the mainsail, but when going downwind, they found it impossible. Jim started the engine to turn Déjà vu against the wind. At that manoeuvre, the procurator fell out of his bunk and woke up. On staggering feet, he got up in the cockpit, screaming,

'What the fuck are you doing?'

He grabbed the wheel, and as Déjà vu turned, a large wave broke over the cockpit, washing both the procurator and Jim overboard. Milan managed to hang on to the rail because he was the only one who was wearing a hooked-up safety line. He got up, grabbed the wheel, and turned the yacht downwind. He saw Jim's head out of the water as he passed the body of the procurator floating head down. Milan could not turn Déjà vu around, but if he had succeeded, it would not be possible for him to recover either of the men washed overboard.

Milan tied himself to the wheel while motoring west. He was dizzy and his muscles were aching after the lightning strike, and he had a headache after the fall backwards in the cockpit. He tried to stand up and look ahead, but the waves were high and washed over the cockpit. The wind pulled Déjà vu forward on the rigging alone. Milan felt he needed to sit down, or even lie down, but he knew he had to steer the yacht. He struggled for at least an hour before he sat on the bench, slowly losing consciousness.

Déjà vu struck the reef with a massive blow. A wave lifted the hull over the reef, and it came down with all its weight. The wave had turned the yacht, so the hit was along the side of the flexible hull. Déjà vu sat hard among the corals with its shredded genoa fluttering in the wind, fifty meters from the edge. Waves did not move the vessel further; it was only bumping up and down. Milan's lifeline firmly secured his body to the wheel.

After a daily visit to the Mango Bar and the cafe across, John and Gladys returned to Sunset Dreaming for an evening cup of coffee, relaxing in the cockpit. Gladys had already been below to check for any messages on her SAT phone. There was one. Her former employer, DEA, the US Drug Enforcement Agency, who owned the phone, informed her they had lost the signal from Déjà vu two weeks ago. They appreciated her observation of the vessel in Niuatoputapu. Still, the Tonga police did not know where the yacht was, but they believed she was heading south, probably anchoring at an outer atoll. Would she, please head south searching for Déjà vu among the many distant atolls? Furthermore, the message read, the officers from MV Simba had been forced into a lifeboat about 200 nautical miles south of Tongatapu Island. The office has requested NOAA to calculate a route of the lifeboat considering the oceanographic conditions. Please assist with their rescue.

When Gladys read the message for John, he shook his head in disbelief and pulled the hair he had left on his upper skull.

'Relax, John, it is exciting. I told you that! Let's pack up and leave at sunrise.'

Yet again, John accepted his fate, and that a life with Gladys was never dull. Early in the morning, Sunset Dreaming left the town of Neiafu on the island of Vava'u. John felt a moment of melancholy as he saw the Mango Bar fade away in the distance.

At the end of the long fjord of Neiafu, they turned south towards the string of windward atolls. They had decided to cruise south with some protection from the outer reef, stretching south for miles. Gladys focused on the islands in the atoll, scanning everyone she saw for mast and sails. John's job was to sail Sunset Dreaming, steering safely among the many leeward reefs; luckily, they were far between.

Most of the leeward islands were uninhabited and covered with coconut trees and Casuarinas. Gladys complained to John that she found the islands monotonously dull but kept up the scanning with binoculars. After sailing 10 nautical miles south, Sunset Dreaming arrived close to a group of windward atolls. There, three or four islands were popping up along the long coral reef, but also a large number protected further west. Gladys pointed at a small, elongated island covered with vegetation.

'John,' she said, 'what's the name of this one?'

John looked at the colour plotter and said, 'They call it Luatafito, and it doesn't look like anybody is living there.'

Gladys pointed again and said, 'Maybe it's our lucky day. I think there is a yacht lying down on the outer reef. I can see something there to the right.'

She handed John the binoculars.

'Yes,' he said, 'you may be right; there is something, maybe a wreck. Let's check it out.'

John carefully navigated Sunset Dreaming close in the lee of the island, but he could not get as close as he wanted. After a bit of discussion, they anchored in a pocket of sand, although John was worried that the wind would cause the anchor to drag. It got quickly deep off the sand pocket. They decided to get in the dinghy, and secure Sunset Dreaming with a smaller anchor dropped among the coral boulders towards the shore.

'I can always snorkel it up if the chain gets entangled.' John said, looking forward to a swim because the coral and the visibility were stunning.

With Gladys equipped with a camera and both with sunscreen and sun hats on, they motored their dinghy carefully over the extensive reef platform towards what they thought was a wrecked sailboat of some kind. When they passed the southern tip of the island, Gladys was sure.

'It is a fairly large yacht laying on its side. It still has a bit of sail fluttering in the wind,' she said, while trying to steady the binoculars.

A swell and waves were coming over the outer reef, and although with reduced height, the waves caused spray to go over the bow of their inflatable dinghy, drenching both Gladys and John. When they got closer, a gross sight met them. It was a 42-foot Beneteau lying on its side with the bow facing east towards open water. The waves lifted the hull up gently and down, and a sizeable hole allowed water to enter and leave the cabin. The impact of the reef had broken half of the skeg rudder off, but the keel was undamaged. Gladys turned to John and said,

'I think we will be out of here soon. There is a sunbaked corpse hanging on the wheel. I will take a few photos, but I think this is a job for the police.'

Gladys took photos, and at the stern, she recognised the name. It was indeed Déjà vu. She looked at John, who appeared somewhat pale as he gazed at the corpse of Milan, and said, 'I think this is real dead reckoning!'

Back on Sunset Dreaming, Gladys dispatched the photographs

and the position of the wreck to her previous employer with a 'good luck'.

While Gladys was below with her phone, John sat, or rather lay, on the cockpit bench, supported by the usual set of pillows and cushions he had been able to claim as his. Starboard site was always where he spent time while Gladys preferred the port side. However, in conditions under sail, where Sunset Dreaming was leaning, Gladys moved freely between the two sides, ignoring any previous unarticulated assumptions. John could not get the sight of Milan's corpse out of his mind. The image had invaded his mind and thoughts in a way that made him feel ready to vomit. Gladys came up and handed him a cup of coffee, which he accepted. John looked at his wife with a feeling of repulsion when she offered him a spam sandwich smudged with hot tomato mayonnaise. He declined and leaned back, feeling worse than a minute ago.

'Suit yourself,' Gladys said and turned her attention to her notebook and a handheld GPS.

The coffee made John feel better, and he could now mobilise interest in Gladys' affairs. 'What are you doing,' he asked, superficially interested.

Without looking up, Gladys reported, 'I got some info from the office; they have been busy. The geodetic department had acquired time using the Landsat in search of the Danish lifeboat. They believe they have found it. The office gave me a position further south of here. It is an uninhabited island called Tonumeia. They say there is a lifeboat there. I have set up a waypoint. The distance is 102 nautical miles and the direction 216 degrees. With the current wind we could be there in 16 hours. Also, a Kiwi rescue vessel is on its way, but I think we will be there first.'

John rolled his eyes and got up murmuring,

'Well then, we better get on our way.'

The four sailors rowed east until they had the island on their starboard side. They could see breakers on the fringe reef. Captain Rasmussen steered the lifeboat towards the reef, and then followed the reef edge at a safe distance.

At one point north of the island, there were no breakers, and he turned the boat south towards the shore.

The rowers were sweating, asking why he was turning.

'I think there is a channel towards land because it's dark blue all the way in,' he answered. Captain Rasmussen took Mester's oar leaving him to steer, and the rowers continued. Mester was still suffering from the blow the guy from Bounty Shipping had inflicted. Slowly they rowed further in, and Mester steered them up to the shallows at the beach. They all jumped into the water, and pulled the boat up on the sand as far as they could.

'What a lovely place,' Styrmand said. 'If there is water, I will stay and make myself a grass skirt.'

They all sat down in the sand, exhausted after all the rowing, but before long they organised themselves.

Coconut was abundant, and Gnisten caught two coconut crabs. There were fishing lines, sinkers, and hooks on the lifeboat, so Skipper and Mester took the lifeboat out in the blue channel, and started fishing using small crabs they caught on the beach as bait. Styrmand dug a hole in the ground and filled it with volcanic stones. He started a fire on top. Styrmand and Gnisten built two shelters with driftwood and covered them with large leaves and other stuff he found. When Skipper and Mester came back, they cleaned the fish and packed them in broad leaves together with the coconut crabs. They had tried to keep the coconut crabs alive, but they were nasty, and Gnisten got a bite he would not soon forget. After that experience, he killed them both. Styrmand extinguished the fire, and all the wrapped seafood was placed on top of the hot stones and covered with leaves and soil. After the meal, and watching the setting sun for a time, the four sailors turned in for the night.

Sunset Dreaming, with Gladys and John onboard, had made progress going south. They stayed west of the northern Hapai Group because of all the navigational hazards they may not spot at night. All the islands south are low, and the south-east trade wind rushed Sunset Dreaming along. At early sunrise, John had Nomuka Island in sight and Sunset Dreaming entered the Southern Hapai Group of islands. When Gladys surfaced from below with two mugs of coffee in her hands, they had Nomuka Island on starboard going straight south.

'Morning Gladys,' John said with a sleepy voice. 'We have Mango Island on our port. I wonder whether they sell draught beer there?'

Gladys shook her head and gave him his mug. There was now open water between Sunset Dreaming and the island of Tonumeia, 12 nautical miles away. John went below after adjusting the windvane and left Gladys to the navigation. After setting the alarm on his watch for an hour, he fell asleep.

John woke up to a banging sound. It was Gladys stomping the boatman's hook on the floor of the cockpit shouting.

'John, get up, we are here!'

John staggered up in the cockpit, instantly blinded by the bright sunlight. She handed him his sunglasses.

John looked at a large fringing reef with an extensive reef platform behind. Gladys had already taken the mainsail down and furled the genoa back. The motor was running. Gladys shook John's shoulder and pointed towards the island.

'Look,' she said, 'there is a deep blue channel going in, and the lifeboat is on the beach. Let's get in; it may be deep enough.'

John had eventually woken up and grabbed the wheel while Gladys got out at the bow, holding on to the furling stay. Slowly, John motored into the channel looking at Gladys who directed him left or right as they progressed. About 100 meters from the shore, Gladys lifted her hand, and as John stopped Sunset Dreaming, she let the anchor go out. It was about five meters deep, and just enough space for Sunset Dreaming to turn around with the wind.

On the beach were four Danish sailors looking at Sunset Dreaming in disbelief. Soon, Gladys and John arrived on the beach in their dinghy.

'Ahoy there!' John said while helping Gladys out.

The four sailors lined up, and with Gladys in front, the couple shook hands as if they were inspecting a tribal welcome committee.

Before long, they had cleared the situation up. Gladys told the sailors that she had agreed to take them onboard Sunset Dreaming and go to Nuku'alofa just 45 nautical miles due south. The Kiwi rescue vessel had turned around when they learned about Sunset Dreaming's proximity to Tonumeia. John soon felt that the four sailors did not really want to leave. It looked like they had settled in on the island. It was only the effects of the sun which seemed to bother them, because they were all wearing something that looked like straw hats on their heads, keeping their sunburned faces in the shade. But a few words from the captain got them going and one by two by two, they were all motored out to Sunset Dreaming.

With all the shipwrecked sailors onboard, John took Sunset Dreaming around Tonumeia and well back in the trade wind. With Gladys at the helm, he got the mainsail up and furled the genoa out. The feeling of speed and being under wind brought smiles to the faces of the Danish sailors. Styrmand got up and asked Gladys whether he could take the wheel after explaining that he had been an instructor and the master of shipowners J. L. Pedersen's school ship, a two-masted topsail schooner sailing in Danish waters called "Lille Peter". Suddenly, Gladys and John sat in the cockpit with nothing to do. The skipper was arguing with

Styrmand over a roster at the wheel. Mester was discussing the engine with John, trying to convince him he may have a problem with one valve of his diesel engine, and that the distributor needed cleaning and adjustment. Gnisten enjoyed the company of Gladys, and in no time, navigational instructions were passed on to Styrmand at the helm.

At dinnertime, Gnisten served freshly cooked coconut crab together with three lobsters he had caught on the reef flat the previous night. They finished the lot and nearly all the fresh vegetables Gladys had onboard.

In the middle of the night, just before the entry to Nuku'alofa, Skipper woke up John and Gladys. Skipper and Styrmand sat together on one of the benches below and looked thoughtfully at the couple opposite.

'What's your problem?' Gladys asked. Styrmand looked down while Skipper looked straight in the eyes of Gladys and temporally on John.

'We have been thinking about our situation. We do not want to go ashore in the Tonga capital after what happened on MV Simba. We do not trust these people, and they probably see us as an inconvenience, considering the possible involvement of the royal court. I will ask you, whether you would be so kind to take us to New Zealand instead?'

Gladys and John did not say anything, so Skipper continued, 'Look at it this way, you will have a qualified crew on board. You two don't even have to be on the roster. We will share bunks because there will always be two on duty. We loaded onboard all the remaining provisions from the lifeboat. Gnisten says that there is enough to reach New Zealand, and you have a water maker, so we will not run out of freshwater. Mester says that he will fish whenever there is an opportunity. We will, of course, compensate you for the inconvenience.'

Gladys looked at John, and without asking him, she immediately responded to the request. 'Of course, we will be delighted to have you onboard.'

1050 nautical miles of problem-free sailing later, Sunset Dreaming entered Waitemata Harbour in Auckland and found the customs dock. It was early in the morning, and they all sat in the cockpit drinking coffee. Gnisten pointed out that it was good that all the provisions on Sunset Dreaming were consumed because now there is no problem with biosecurity. They were all happy, and Gladys and John had enjoyed the sailing, which had been effortless and exciting. They were impressed with both Skipper and Styrmand who had demonstrated their skills and got speed and pleasurable sailing out of Sunset Dreaming they had never experienced before. Mester had changed the oil and filter on the engine while under sail, cleaned the troublesome valve, and the injectors as well. Gladys was impressed with Gnisten and his recipes. She had never seen so many delicious meals coming out of cans of food, many she had never seen before. Gnisten also cleaned up her computer, which was getting sluggish, and taught both her and John more about their HF radio, which they had only used a little since Gladys brought the SAT phone onboard.

The customs dock came to life about nine. Then somebody was knocking on the hull, and a voice shouted, 'Permission to come on board?'

John looked out of the cockpit at a stranger.

'Yes, please come on board,' he answered.

Shipowner Knud Pedersen entered the cockpit, and the four sailors jumped up from their seat.

'Sit down! Don't tilt the boat; I may get seasick!' he cried.

They all laughed.

Gladys offered Knud a seat so they all could fit in. She served him a mug of coffee. 'Welcome to New Zealand,' Knud said with a slightly nervous smile. 'I'm so pleased to see you all again.

I hope you have enjoyed the adventure. Lucy has booked you an open first-class ticket and rooms on the Airport Kiwi Hotel, so everything is ready for your return.'

Knud turned to John and Gladys and said, 'I appreciate your rescue of my officers; it was a marvellous effort. I thought you would have off-loaded my officers in Tongatapu?'

'No, we would not do that,' Gladys said with a little smile. 'Your officers and others have taught us a little about dead reckoning!'

The Danish ship officers packed up the little they had and thanked and hugged Gladys and John. Mester had tears in his eyes. Knud Pedersen shook John's hand and kissed Gladys on her cheek while handing her an envelope with the bright red and white logo of J. L. Pedersen Shipping. After the departure of Danish sailors, John and Gladys sat down in the cockpit, feeling a bit sad to see their newfound friends go.

Gladys opened the envelope. It contained a cheque for $20,000 and a folded card with the J. L. Pedersen Shipping logo and a text "With Compliments". In the folded card were two tickets, always giving free passage on all J. L. Pedersen Shipping's vessel. John had a look and smiled at Gladys and said, 'I think that trips on those cargo vessels will not be a dead reckoning!'

Extracts from the Log of a cruising yacht

Friday, July 6

It is Julie's birthday. We left for Luganville on Espiritu Santo with 20 knots SE wind. Enjoyable sailing: Aeolus ran at 7.5 knots. We lost a lure with the steel wire cut — some big fish around here! We anchored at Luganville waterfront. Difficult place with a tide running and waves along the coast.

Saturday, July 7

We moved across the Second Strait to Aore Resort and hooked up to a mooring — too deep for anchoring. We had dinner at the resort. I rowed the dinghy back with our guest, Heather, and my wife, Yadranka, sitting on the tubes. It was a flat, calm, starry night. Suddenly, a forceful spray of water drenched us. I saw the tail of a large shark. In seconds, the port side tube deflated, the two ladies clinging in fear to the starboard one. We managed to get back to the dock. An inspection revealed a large hole forward. Staff from the resort got us back on Aeolus. Friendly people on the cat "Caballito De Mar" gave us glue and a large PVC sheet.

Saturday, October 20

We spent the week on anchor at Huon Reef, New Caledonia. It was blowing 20 knots+ all the time. Weather elsewhere was the same, and towards New Zealand periodically very bad. A cruiser was dismasted off the NSW coast when on his way to NZ. We had the company of "Attitude" with Neil and Kathy onboard and the cat "Two Companions" with Steven and Vicky. Friendly people, and we were introduced to "Mexican Train Domino". The "Grib File" three day forecast show less wind towards Chesterfield Reef, so we decided to leave. The forecast says that after three days, the wind will again pick up to 25 knots+. By then, we hope to be safely anchored in the Chesterfield Reef lagoon.

Sunday, October 21

A hard day and night in 20 knots wind from SE, rolling waves, but beautiful sailing. We did 6-6.5 knots on the rag of a genoa and the trysail in the main. Caught up with "Attitude" during early morning. Log 8285 NM, course 230°T. 154 NM to Chesterfield. Had contact with P2P radio "Fred" at 06.15 AEST. There were lots of boats on their way to Bundaberg.

Monday, October 22

At 3 in the afternoon, wind dropped a bit, which made the night sailing quite nice. We travelled at 5.5 knots all night, riding on a swell. At sunrise, I fished again. We had P2P radio contact with "Fred" at 6.15 about 20 NM from Chesterfield Reef. On approach to the lagoon, we caught a 16-pound Trevally — nice fish. We motored south to Les Trois Islet and anchored at 23 feet of water. Log 8443 NM. We had traveled 158 NM since yesterday and 279 NM in two days without motoring. This is pretty good for Aeolus on a reduced genoa and a trysail.

Saturday, October 27

Spend a few days at Les Trois in the company of "Attitude", "True Companions", and a Kiwi boat with a difficult name. It was blowing 20 knots+ from S-SE, making the anchorage a bit difficult. A weather window, so we are leaving for Bundaberg at 09.30 in the morning.

Sunday, October 28

A night with good winds out of SE reaching 22 knots. At one stage, we did 8 knots plus. Somewhat difficult to trim the boat to 220°, but we got it going. Radio contact last night was a joke because P2P could not hear anybody, but we could hear him and everybody else. Position at 09.00 AEST, 21°10' S; 157° 02' E. Course 220°, speed 6.3 knots wind variable 15 knots; rough seas. Log 8561 NM. We have travelled 117 NM since yesterday. A front is established off the Queensland coast moving SE to 22° S. We can expect 20 knots wind and rain.

Monday, October 29

Bad weather came down upon us. The Grib Files were constantly changing and a front that was shown to the south suddenly came north. The front brought strong, cold winds and rain. At 03.00 in the morning, we had 25 knots+ wind from SE and four-meter waves. The monitor had to be adjusted regularly, forcing us a bit out of course. Sails were reduced to minimum. Course 268°T. We had done 158 NM in 24 hours. Sufficient sleep is a problem. Checked in on P2P radio at 06.15 AEST. There were a few boats around us, all heading to Bundaberg. The Grip files say that the 25 knot+ winds will last until tomorrow.

Tuesday, October 30

Arrived at the quarantine buoy at Burnett Head at 05.30 in the afternoon. Log 8907 NM. During the night, a cat got into trouble. Captain and a young family crew were lifted out by a helicopter.

We have now completed our trans-Pacific passage, which began on March 27, 2011, and ended October 30, 2013. The longest passage was from La Cruz, Mexico, to the Marquesas Islands, 2852 NM. It took us 24 days. We didn't see a single boat.

Cape Town to Fremantle

My friends and I met every Friday afternoon at the Norfolk Hotel in Fremantle. It was a simple after-work event after a long week. We had a couple of beers and then dispersed home or elsewhere.

I was a junior journalist at the Fremantle Herald. It was an exciting job, and coming to Norfolk gave me an extra kick because it was a meeting place for many professionals in the town. People came from Perth, and there were always gossips to pick up.

The Dockers were playing, so my friends drifted into the gambling room where the big television was. I was not keen on footy and stayed at the bar, wondering whether I should go home to my apartment or stay on. I could try calling a girlfriend, but I did not have any close. The truth is I did not have a girlfriend at all.

I looked around at the tables in the room, and an older man caught my attention. He sat in a corner by himself with a pint of beer in front of him. There was nothing remarkable about his appearance except for his clothes. He wore a wool sweater of a kind I have seen before and dark blue trousers. He had a typical Scandinavian skipper cap in dark navy blue. His sweater was in distinct Norwegian hand-knitted patterns, which I remembered as a child. My grandparents were Norwegian, and my parents, my sister and I visited the family in Norway many times.

Meeting people of a similar origin can be emotional. It's like searching for something missed in childhood without knowing exactly what. I decided to say hello.

I said, 'Sorry to disturb you, but I could not resist the temptation. Are you Norwegian?'

He said nothing, opened his hand, and moved his arm a little to the right like saying, 'Please sit down.'

I sat across from him and expected a conversation to start, but he said nothing. I looked at his wind-beaten face and rough hands and asked, 'Are you a sailor?'

He gave a deep sigh and said, 'No, not really. You may call me a yachtsman, but I'm a carpenter as a profession.'

Then he paused, and I didn't know how to continue our conversation. I decided to talk about myself. 'My grandparents were Norwegians; they have passed away. We still have family in Norway, but not many anymore. Have you been to Norway?'

The old man looked at me and, in a low voice, said, 'I have lived in Norway most of my adult life, but I was born in Fremantle. When I was eighteen, my uncle invited me to Norway to be an apprentice in his business in Stavanger on the coast. I did not know what to do after school, so it was an adventure for me. I accepted, not knowing whether my father would pay for the ticket. But he did. I suspect that he was happy to see me off.'

'I know Stavanger,' I said. 'I have been there only once because we were always in Oslo.'

The older man nodded as if he understood the difference between people from Oslo and the people from Stavanger. There are many dialects in Norway, and the Stavanger has its own, just like other places further north along the coast.

The old man nodded and said, 'I was happy for the

apprenticeship, and my uncle was great. There was a lot of work. Timber was plentiful; we built timber houses. Life passed quickly, and before long, I was married. Unfortunately, we did not have any children.'

A deep sigh followed, and he continued, 'My wife passed away in her early fifties. Suddenly I was alone. I could not accept that she was dead, and a deep sorrow overwhelmed me. After being on the bottle for a while, I decided to go back to Fremantle. I still had my parents here and my sister.'

The old man appeared vitalised by the thought of his parents and sister and continued. 'I had a boat, a ketch I had built myself. It was my pride and joy. So, I sold our house and the lot, packed the boat, and left. It was autumn, but I managed to avoid the usual storms and sailed to the Canary Islands. I crossed over to Brazil and stayed for a while before heading south. I followed the old sailing routes. I called in at St. Helena in the South Atlantic, and after a messy passage, I arrived in Cape Town. The stormy weather had not been kind to "The Fulmar," which was the name of my boat.'

I sat in silence, listening to the older man, happy that he was telling me his story. I thought it was better to let him tell his story undisturbed.

I looked at his glass, which now was empty. I asked, 'Would you like another beer?'

He nodded. I went up to the bar feeling worried that he might not continue. Back at the table, he looked happily at his pint, held it up, looked at me and said, 'skål', the Scandinavian expression for "cheers".

He leaned back against the wall and looked at me as if searching for something. I smiled and asked, 'Did you sail directly to Fremantle?'

'Sort of, yes, but not really,' he answered. 'You see, one day in Cape Town, someone came to the dock and knocked on the cabin roof when I was below. A voice said, "Hello, anyone home?" I got up in the cockpit and saw a tall, strong-looking man in his late forties standing on the dock, looking at me. Like you, I noticed his clothes looked traditional Norwegian. I said, "hello."'

'He looked closely up and down at the boat and said, "I hear you are going to Fremantle. Can I join you as a crew?" "I am not sure about that," I said, "but I will give it some thought and let you know." I asked, "what's your name?" "My name is Sigurd Halfdan. I'm a sailor myself, but I understand. I will come later when you have thought about it." He walked away.'

After a pause, the old man continued,

'Needless to say, but I was worried. It's at least a thirty-day trip to Fremantle and being on a boat with a person onboard you do not know can be disastrous. But there was something attractive about him. He certainly gave the appearance of being a skilled sailor. You can always tell. His Norwegian name appealed to me.'

The old man fell into deep thoughts, had a sip of his beer, and continued, 'The next day, he came back, and I told him I would accept him as a crew but with no pay. I gave him some stern words about the duties I expected him to carry out. He accepted with a big smile. He seemed happy with my decision.

'We left the following day, and Sigurd impressed me with his sailing skills and knowledge. I was delighted to get some sleep and leave the responsibility of sailing to him. We had agreed to four hours shift all the way. It turned out to be easy sailing. Like the Dutch hundreds of years ago, we followed the 36-degree latitude straight east, and we had good wind from the south-west, sometimes 25 knots, but no more. The Fulmar was flying.'

The old man paused and had a sip of his beer, then he continued, 'After two weeks of sailing west, we ran into rain and sometimes fog. That didn't bother us too much. Then Sigurd was looking intensively east with the binoculars and said, "I think we have an island ahead." "Can I have a look?" I said, and he handed me the set. I looked through the rainy mist, and there was without doubt something ahead that looked like an island. "I cannot understand this," I said to Sigurd. "There is not supposed to be an island where we are!"'

The old man looked at me as if he was worried, but continued, 'I opened the plotter, and sure enough, there was an island, but only on the largest scale and only as an outline — no details at all. At a smaller scale, there was nothing. I suggested to Sigurd that we better have a close look. He agreed with a smile. We sailed closer, and there were birds everywhere. Albatrosses, petrels and skuas were flying around. The island was volcanic with black sand on the beach, and on the northern side, the home to a herd of elephant seals. We got into a bay with a slight swell and looked for a possible anchorage. Then Sigurd said, "I think there is a passage leading further in!" Sure enough, we motored through a wide entrance into a circular bay, and in front of us we saw old, grey, wind worn-wooden buildings and rusty iron tanks, possibly the remains of an old whaling station because there were large whale bones on the beach. There were also rusty ribs, the remains of a beached ship.'

'Sigurd was at the bow, and he pointed towards the foothills. I stopped the boat and had a look through the binoculars. There were several grey wooden houses. The windows seemed to be complete, some with curtains. Then Sigurd eagerly pointed towards the houses. I looked closely, wondering what his excitement was all about. Then I saw people coming out, and children were playing. The adults stopped and stood like statues staring at us. Sigurd returned to the cockpit and said, "There are people here. We should go ashore."'

I looked at the old man and nodded a bit to ensure he knew he had all my attention, so he continued, 'We anchored, and after a light meal, we got the dinghy with an outboard into the water and motored to the sandy shore. We slowly started to walk toward the houses, but the terrain was not easy and took time. After a while, we stopped and looked. There were still people there, but the children had gone, and as we approached further, the few remaining adults disappeared. Then Sigurd suggested I should go back to the boat so one would be on board if anything unexpected happened. He would continue his own and come back later. I understood his concern and went back to the boat. Sigurd disappeared among the rocks towards the houses. Back on the boat, I had a cup of tea and a rest on the bunk.'

'Later, I heard Sigurd call from the beach. I got in the dinghy to fetch him and saw a relatively young lady dressed in Norwegian wool garments waiting a good distance behind Sigurd as I approached the beach. She stood still. Sigurd said, "I have had an invitation. I will stay ashore for the night and return to the boat tomorrow. I hope you will accept?"'

'What could I say? He had obviously got female companionship. It is not my business, and we had already decided to stay the night. Sigurd walked towards the lady, and I got back in the dinghy.'

There was a pause, and I felt that the older man wanted to stop his narrative. I may have looked interested enough, so he continued, 'The next morning, I woke up after a good sleep, and at the early sunrise, I saw Sigurd coming down the hill from the houses, and about a hundred meters behind was his faithful lady. Onshore, Sigurd told me he would not join me any further. He would stay on the island. He apologised but said that he hoped I would respect his decision. I expressed concern about living in such a remote place, but he insisted that it would be no problem. He came from a small island in the Lofoten group in northern Norway. He assured me he was used to living on isolated islands. What more could I say? I said goodbye, thanked him for all the help and good weather he had brought and sailed away. I would be in Fremantle in ten days or so.'

Now I could see that the older man's story had become a burden for him. His facial expression was sorrowful, and his eyes were watering a little, which could be his tears, or maybe from the hotel air. He nevertheless continued, 'The weather remained fine, and the sailing was fine. I encountered no gales but occasionally brief strong winds. Ten days later, I arrived in Fremantle and moored at the customs dock with the yellow flag on the mast. My VHF radio had died, so I could not call the customs, but I was sure they would see me when I arrived. Within a short time, two officers arrived and climbed onboard.'

'Below, they went through the papers, and they checked my passport. Then the officer in charge said, "I see that you had a crew on board. What happened to him?" I pointed to the customs entry form and said, "He decided to stay on an island at that position. People were living there. I handed his passport back, but I have the number. His name is Sigurd Halfdan. He is a Norwegian citizen."'

'It was like the customs officers wanted me to confirm what they already knew from going through the papers. The junior officer wrote the number in his notebook and went ashore. A short time later, two police officers in civilian clothes arrived. I was wondering what it was all about. The two officers started to question me about Sigurd, and I told them the story. They repeated an annoying question several times, "Are you sure that Sigurd did not fall overboard or had a misfortune on the island?" I answered no and repeated that he wanted to be left behind with a woman.'

'Both officers shook their heads in disbelief. Then they changed the subject, and one of them asked, "So where is this island of yours?" I gave them the position and said that this was all I knew. I told them that the outline of the island was in the plotter. Encouraged, I started the plotter and looked for the waypoint I had placed when we were on anchor. To my surprise, the island had gone, completely disappeared from the electronic map, but my waypoint was there! The two police officers went back to the customs building, and after a while, another man, looking like a doctor, arrived with my sister. I had not seen her for years, and it was an emotional reunion. We both cried.'

'The doctor sat down next to the senior customs officer and said, "I'm a doctor because the police have concerns about your health, but to me, you look all right!" I was puzzled. Then he said, "I have to ask you some questions. The customs have checked the passport number of Sigurd Halfdan as you provided. It is correct that a Norwegian passport with that number had been issued to Mr. Sigurd Halfdan, but he is listed as deceased, lost at sea. What do you say about that?"'

'I said that I didn't know. When I left him, he was alive and well. "But you see," the doctor said, "he was lost from a Norwegian fishing vessel twenty years ago!"'

'"Well," I said. "It must be an error. As I said, he was alive and well when I left him. You have it all, dates, and positions in the logbook."'

'The custom officer and the doctor stared at me while my sister held my hand. It was getting very uncomfortable. The custom officer looked at me harshly and said, "Then, where did you go, and why did it take six years to sail from Cape Town to Fremantle? Explain that?" I was stunned.'

The older man was crying a bit, and I felt sorry for him. I placed my hand on his shoulder and said, 'I understand you. You can only tell the truth as you see it, not what other people are guessing.'

Never had I heard such a story before.

He cheered up a bit when I gave him a fresh beer, and I asked, 'What happened to you afterwards?'

'I was taken away by the police and the doctor. The doctor thought I was mad and tried to put me into an asylum. I must admit that my behaviour at that point was a bit odd after being exposed to the customs, the doctor, and the police questioning.

Still, my sister got me out because they could not prove anything about Sigurd going missing. A Norwegian coroner had already dealt with this earlier.

My sister brought me to her home. She told me that our parents had passed away four years ago, one after another. She also showed me what day it was, and surely enough, I had been sailing between Cape Town and Fremantle for six years.'

Islanders and Landlubbers

There are many islands in the archipelago along the Swedish west coast. It's a rocky coast, and the islands are mostly granite, with little land available for agriculture. Even a small veggie patch needs protection from salt and wind. Some potatoes can be grown for an early harvest. People who earlier lived there were tough and sustained themselves through fishing. Dried cod and salted herrings provided an income, but it was a hard life. Today most of the older cottages have been taken over by summer guests, who enjoy a few months of fair weather and temperature. An island cottage is expensive, so only rich people can afford such a luxury. A sarcastic visitor once said that in our time islanders sustain themselves by baiting the property owners' rat traps.

During the summertime, the temporarily inhabited islands may have a ferry connection to the mainland towns, which are bustling with tourists eager to absorb the air, the sun, and the sea. The ferrymen are locals, who always look forward to the extra seasonal income. When not on ferry duty, off time is used for mackerel fishing, a fish that is abundant during the summer and appreciated by the locals and summer guests alike. Surplus mackerels and rock crabs are traded in the informal economy.

In earlier times, connection to the mainland was by fishing

boat. either rowed or sailed. The islander's boats were small, one masted wooden vessels, skillfully crafted using the abundance of oak and lark found in the forests sloping down to the shore of the deep fjords. Boatbuilding here has a long tradition maintained for thousands of years. Earlier, larger wooden vessels were built at the many shipyards along the coast. But the interest for these vessels has waned in favour of steel, aluminum, or fiberglass. In modern times, boat building along the coast is restricted to yacht manufacturing, usually taking place in small inland towns reached by the long fjords.

Still, the boat building tradition lives on. Among the locals, there is little disagreement about what constitutes a beautiful boat, and such a boat will always be seaworthy and a pleasure to the skilled eye. It is in their veins, deeply rooted in the Viking tradition and even earlier. In many places, extensive rock carvings show, among other things, Viking style ships with large crews. These carvings date back to 1800 BC.

Along the coast, the landscape is dotted with easily recognisable navigation markers of unknown age. Just like in Norway and Scotland, they are cone-shaped piles of rocks guiding sailors through the archipelago. Vandalism of these markers is rare, and if it occurs, they are quickly resurrected, even in our time of electronic navigation tools. Before the appearance of GPS, the approach to the Swedish archipelago was difficult without the markers. Attempting the approach at night was indeed risky without a keen navigational knowledge of the coast, the lighthouses, and their characteristics. Needless to say, in poor weather, sailors with no local experience stayed offshore.

The Swedish church has always had a stronghold among the local coast population. The church was exposed to the Middle Age Reformation but didn't change. It still has a Catholic appearance, and in contrast to elsewhere in Europe, the church kept their large landholdings and money. Priests wear an outfit like their Catholic counterparts. Sects of different kinds are abundant. Many preach a strong Pietistic faith. A Saturday visit to the town of Lysekil is essential for many outsiders because here you will find the only available bottle shop called "Systembolaget". Visitors are likely to be confronted by locals, asking you a tautological question in their easily recognisable dialect. 'Have you met Jesus?'

The visitor may answer, 'How do I know?'

An explanation will quickly but quietly follow. 'When you have met Jesus, you will know!'

The island of Gåsö (Goose Island), just southwest of the town of Lysekil. It is a moderately large island — a beautiful place. In springtime, it is magical. In early March, the first oystercatchers arrive after a long journey from Africa. In early May, the eider ducks start nesting, hiding between the rocks, and everywhere the sea thrifts are flowering, providing impressive carpets of pink. The spring air, mixed with the scent of flowers and the ocean beyond, generates a mild intoxication that will never leave your memory. In Lysekil, I once overheard a conversation between two young women, 'When you fall in love, even Gåsö is liveable!'

One day in spring, a boat from Gåsö came to a small bay, Gåsevig, on the western side of Skaftö, an island towards the east connected to the mainland by a bridge. The boat was traditionally rigged and carried a man and his young son. I later learned that the man was a fisher living on Gåsö. He and his family had lived on the island for generations. They were on their way to the Skaftö supermarket, recently expanded from a small in-town grocery to a large modern shop, just outside town; the consequence of an influx of 3000 or so summer guests, supplementing the about 400 permanent residents.

Securing their boat, the father and son followed a narrow path from the bay leading to the main road. In doing so, they passed a paddock with two horses. The horses were friendly and familiar with visitors. They were pony-sized riding horses, brought in by a summer visitor, probably to entertain his daughters.

The son stopped in his tracks and stared, somewhat bewildered.

'Daddy,' he asked in a strong dialect, 'are they horses?'

His father replied in the same dialect. 'Yes, my son, they surely are.'

Both father and son appreciated the horses, fed them grass, and patted the horses' necks and foreheads. One horse was more approachable, which quickly became the favourite. The son was unsure and wary of the teeth. The father explained to his son,

'When you feed a horse, always open your palm, and let the horse feed on your open hand. Then he will not bite you!'

Convinced by the friendliness of the horses, the father climbed over the fence. He stood next to the horses, who didn't seem to mind. The son followed, encouraged by his father.

After a while, the son asked, 'Can I ride this horse?'

The father answered, 'Yes, I suppose you can. Just step up in my folded hands, and I will help you up.'

The son quickly followed the instructions of his father and swiftly was on the back of the horse. The horse raised its head and started to stroll along. The son grabbed hold of the mane, looking a bit surprised.

The horse moved along in a light trot, circling the father while the other horse was looking on.

The son was in fear, holding on to the mane as best as he could.

The father looked on, not knowing how to handle an unexpected situation.

Still trotting, the horse took off with the son hanging on. In a panic, the son cried, 'Daddy, Daddy, how can I stop him?'

A few seconds passed, feeling like minutes, and the father shouted back, 'What do I know — try to steer him into the wind!'

Man Knows Little

A Viking longship was found in a large burial mound at the Oseberg farm in 1904, not far from Tønsberg in Vestfold County, Norway. Oseberg in Old Norse means Ásmountain, the Burial Mound of the Æsir.

The ship is believed to have been buried in 830 AD. It is a beautiful seaworthy longship, 71 feet long, with ornamental carvings fit for a prominent chieftain. In the burial chamber, two female skeletons were found, which was seen as exceptional at its excavation. Even more intriguing was the finding of a runic inscription. The runes had been etched into a piece of wood over two meters long, believed to be a part of an oar, a mast, or of the ship's prow. It read "litet-vis maðr" translated to "man knows little". Rune inscriptions are seen as "a play with words," bragging about an individual's exploits, presenting a challenge to others, or for protection to ward off the evil eye.

Vikings travelled far, and home comers bragged about their findings, especially about new lands, encouraging others to follow. In contrast, the Latin warning "Ne plus ultra — there is nothing further beyond", is believed to be the inscription on the Pillars of Hercules at the Strait of Gibraltar. The "Man Knows Little" inscription, found in a majestic Viking longship, can be an invitation or a challenge issued by the women buried there. It could also be old age wisdom, a reflection of a lived life. But being found in a Viking longship, the inscription can only be a challenge; follow my lead and go beyond because we need to know more.

Scandinavians have always been sailors. Although modern times have made life on the shore more attractive, the basic needs for maritime exploration, the understanding of boats, navigation, and the art of sailing with the winds, is deeply rooted in most. The Scandinavians wander restlessly around in their winter-warm dwellings, waiting for the light and the migrating birds to return.

The oystercatcher arrives from the south in early March. The restlessness becomes unbearable, but Easter is the first sign showing a break. Tarps are taken off the boats, and suddenly a feeling of purpose returns. Boatyards are busy. Boats are washed, aired, and fresh coats of antifouling paint is applied. Sails are inspected, repaired, and hoisted up the mast to be checked. Over a beer or two, old adventures are retold, and new plans are hatched, where to go this year? Not much different from Viking times. By May, most keelboats are in the water.

In the wait for the summer vacation, weekends are used to test the boats to prepare for the summer cruise. For most yachties, a family cruise along the coast, visiting the many natural harbours, is an option. A visit to the fishing village, Smögen, on the Swedish West Coast is a highlight. A trip to Skagen, a fishing village on Jutland's northern tip of Denmark, is always in the plans, and even further to the Isle of Skye, Scotland. The latter cruise is likely to be without mothers and young children. It is a trip for fathers, grown-up daughters, and sons. Many take the inshore route through the crowded Swedish West Coast archipelago and finally enjoy a sleep-over at Väderöarna, the windward islands, to hear the waves break and be rocked to sleep by a light swell. By August, the cruising season is over, and most are back to work. At that time, the offshore cruisers depart, going south to the Canary Islands for an Atlantic passage to the Caribbean and further. A likely once in a lifetime voyage.

Hans Erik was married to Grethe. They had two children, Jacob and Anne Mette, and lived in Elsinore, north of Copenhagen, where the Øresund meets the Kattegat, the gateway to the world. Hans Erik had always dreamed about owning a sailing yacht, but his life had been busy and money for a large investment was not forthcoming. Grethe was not particularly supportive of Hans Erik's dreams. For her, the sea was too dangerous, and her concerns were always for their children. As a matter of fact, she had never been at sea disregarding an occasional ferry trip across the Great Belt.

When the family visited the mighty Elsinore Castle where a statue of a mythological Viking, Holger Danske, or Ogier the Dane, sleeps in the cellar, they watched ships of many nationalities passing north and south. There were yachts, fishing boats and ferries crisscrossing the narrow straight between Denmark and Sweden. It was there Hans Erik's dreams were the strongest. During a visit to the old battery bastion, it became unbearable. He had to think about something else and it was not about Shakespeare's famous tragedy, Hamlet, Prince of Denmark. No, he was thinking about his childhood hero, Tordenskjold, or Peter Wessel, a Danish-Norwegian vice-admiral who fought against the Swedes with great courage in the Great Northern War.

Grethe knew in advance what would happen when Hans Erik and their two children were looking across the Sound; she could see it in his eyes and facial expression. She had packed lunch and quickly organised a blanket for them to sit on in the green grass. Coffee and sandwiches appeared while Hans Erik began telling his children the tales of Tordenskjold's exploits. For Grethe, it was like listening to an old record, but she enjoyed a picnic with her family; their children, Jacob, and Anne Mette, were good listeners.

'Can you imagine,' Hans Erik began while looking firmly at his son. 'Peter Wessel was a wild, unruly boy who gave his parents much trouble.'

'So what?' Jacob yawned impatiently.

'Well,' Hans Erik continued, 'in 1704, at an age of fourteen, he left his hometown of Trondheim in Norway as a stow-away on a vessel bound for Copenhagen. Peter wanted to be a navy cadet and to follow in the footsteps of his uncle, who was a Rear-Admiral. But Peter did not have any success, until a family friend, who was the king's chaplain, helped him. He signed him on to a bunk on a merchant vessel bound for a Danish fort in Guinea on the West Coast of Africa. The ship carried gunpowder, arms, and Danish "snaps" to trade in exchange for slaves. They sailed the slaves to the Danish Virgin Islands in the Caribbean to work in the cane fields. There, they loaded cane sugar and sailed back to Copenhagen.'

Hans Erik paused, looking up at a Russian bulk carrier passing into the sound blowing her horn to warn a ferry.

'Was that it?' Jacob asked.

Hans Erik smiled and continued, 'No, Peter Wessel was also sent to the East Indies, which was a long trip. Denmark had a trading station with a fort at Tranquebar on the Coromandel Coast of East India. Tordenskjold became a real sailor and when he returned, he got a vacant cadetship. Eventually, he was appointed Second Lieutenant in the Royal Danish-Norwegian navy as the captain of a 4-gun sloop Ormen, or HMS Serpent. He was only twenty-one years old.'

'That's old!' Jacob exclaimed.

Anne Mette and Grethe were smiling.

Hans Erik shook his head while looking at his son and continued. 'The Great Northern War was on, and his courage and seamanship was appreciated. He soon found himself a captain of an 18-gun frigate, Løvendals Galej, joining Admiral Gyldenløve in the Baltic Sea. Peter Wessel had gained a reputation for the audacity with which he attacked any Swedish vessel he came across, regardless of the odds. But most of all, his unique seamanship was admired because it enabled him to always evade capture.'

Grethe started to pack up cutlery and finished the last coffee from the thermos. Hans Erik knew that it was time to go home.

'I will tell you more about Tordenskjold next time,' he said with a disappointed look on his face.

When the family arrived home, there was a letter from a Copenhagen lawyer in their letterbox. Hans Erik was nervous because he did not know what to expect, but to his surprise, he learned he had received an inheritance, and it was not a trivial amount. His uncle had died, and the family had attended the funeral in Copenhagen months ago but did not expect anything in the way of an inheritance. It was a complete surprise, and it sent Hans Erik's brain into a spin. Maybe, just maybe, he could get what he had always dreamed about, a sailing yacht. He knew that Grethe would oppose great expenditures and certainly on a sailing yacht. To Hans Erik's surprise, she did not, but asked him cautiously to consider his aspirations carefully, and so he did.

Hans Erik piled up yacht magazines on his desk, read about all the Danish built yachts available, and checked second-hand prices. The task absorbed him for weeks. Eventually, he focused on the Grinde, a monohull double-ended sailboat designed and built by a Mr. Peter Bruun. His factory had ceased production in 1989, so Hans Erik started to look for newer second-hands ones. The Grinde was not a luxury yacht, but a sturdy vessel considered reasonably fast because it had a short keel with a draft of 1.7 m and a skeg rudder. It was 8.2 m (27 feet) long with a broad beam, making the cabin comfortably spacious. Hans Erik admired the shape and lines of the vessel with its broad, strong looking prow and smooth deck, a design that fully lived up to its name, Grinde, or pilot whale. There was something Nordic in the design, and it indicated the Faeroe Islands where the name Grinde came from. There was room enough for four people, the two children in the forepeak and two bunks midships for the adults. What Grethe appreciated was the separate toilet and wardrobe.

In late August, Hans Erik's agent called and told him he had located a Grinde for sale which was likely to suit him. The agent pointed out that it was best to buy yachts in the autumn because sellers did not want the hassle of winter storage and the spring round of antifouling painting. The vessel, built in 1987, was in a small provincial town in Jutland. Hans Erik did not hesitate. He met with the agent. Together, they drove to Jutland and located the owner and marina in the small town of Sønderborg on the island of Als.

When Hans Erik saw the boat, he gaped with amazement. It was light grey with a white deck. It appeared as new and had, according to the owner, only been used for weekends. It had sailed very little. The boat was meticulously maintained. Hans Erik did what he had been told to do: that was to shut up and leave the negotiation to the agent. Finally, an agreement was reached which satisfied everyone. Hans Erik was over the moon.

Autumn and the usual bad weather had arrived in full force, so the agent organised for the boat to be trucked to Elsinore and put on the hard in the marina. Hans Erik couldn't wait to show the boat to Grethe. Eventually, the boat arrived, and she had a brief but pleasing look at the interior before it was put to its winter sleep like a baby in a cradle.

Hans Erik did not waste time. He had already joined the local yacht club and with vigour engaged himself in an inshore yacht skipper course. He passed the exam with distinction. Everybody in the yacht club agreed he had got the best boat on the market, barely hiding their envy. Spring could not come soon enough.

A summer plan slowly emerged by careful negotiation. Anne Mette and Jacob were keen on going and the more adventurous the better. Grethe looked for sunshine, relaxation in calm waters and natural harbours. She had already purchased books to read.

Hans Erik worked over Christmas and Easter securing a full

seven weeks' vacation starting in midsummer when school was over. They decided to join a couple of weekend regattas in the yacht club before departing and then to sail north along the Swedish west coast as far north as Marstrand and Hjerteröen, well known natural harbours. Hans Erik was keen on showing his family Carlsten's fortress at Marstrand because he had a story to tell about Tordenskjold's achievements. His suggestion was met with stoic resignation.

Then Hans Erik took out a card he had kept up in his sleeve. He suggested that Grethe and Anne Mette should, after three weeks, take the train from Göteborg to Elsinore, leaving Jacob with him to sail across the Kattegat to a group of small islands close to the Danish coast called Hirsholmene. There were two islands, but he did not bother explaining that. Hans Erik argued his case that it was a son and father thing, and after three weeks in a confined space he predicted that the two girls would be fed up. He suggested the girls visited the grandparents on the island of Fyn and that they might catch up with them when they go south, just for an eyeball event. The family car was at their disposal. The two girls had no problem accepting the offer, and Grethe gave Anne Mette a wry blink with her eye. She was already looking forward to refreshing their summer wardrobe. They all agreed to rename the boat "Pitter", another Norwegian spelling of the name Peter or Peder, the first name of Tordenskjold. The girls considered the name too masculine and argued that boats are female by tradition. But eventually they agreed that Pitter appeared to be a male, and the name stuck.

Their spring preparations went well, and the family enjoyed the weekend regattas in the yacht club and the many new friends. The boat had an unrealistic budget but eventually, spending stopped when the water line was below the surface. They were ready. On an early morning in sunshine with a light south-westerly breeze, the family onboard Pitter headed north. They sailed in fair weather and stopped at many small coastal places before reaching the entrance to the Swedish Archipelago just south of Göteborg. Hans Erik had previously acquired a chart book from the Swedish Cruising Club, loaded with guides and information about natural harbours along the way north.

The family was emotional when they eventually arrived at Marstrandsön and moored in a marina below Carlsten's fortress. They all felt the pleasure of a family achievement and decided to celebrate with a dinner out and a large ice cream. The following day, Hans Erik mustered his children for a visit to the fortress, which they duly accepted. Grethe stayed behind with a book and in the company of a Norwegian lady from the neighbouring boat.

Hans Erik, Jacob, and Anne Mette joined a guided tour of the fortress. They were lectured in stringent Swedish about the magnificent Swedish Empire under Charles XII. It was an endless bragging about the Swedish victories during the Great Northern War. The guide had realised that his audience was primarily Danes and Norwegians and used the opportunity to firmly establish the Swedish nation as superior in Scandinavia, a view not shared by its neighbours. After listening to the tirade of historical misconceptions, a tall stout Norwegian had had enough and said, 'Tell us about Peter Wessel when he captured the Marstrand fortress and blew up the Gothenburg Squadron.'

The guide swallowed a lump in his throat and his face turned red. It was clear that he was not going to give up without a fight and said, 'The fall of Carlsten's fortress was merely a tactical ploy without any consequence for the outcome of the war. Remember that the fortress commander, Colonel Henrich Danckwardt, was sentenced to death for his cowardly surrender, which he did unauthorised. The ploy was to occupy the Dano-Norwegian forces allowing progress elsewhere, and you took the bait!'

Now the historical conversation had become personal. The Norwegian man got agitated and shouted, 'This colonel, he was German, wasn't he? Why is that you Swedes always mingle cosily with das Wehrmacht? I am just asking.'

The guide's face turned into a grimace, and he tried to force his way through the crowd with clinched fists. Now Hans Erik joined in and shouted, 'Why is that you Swedes never can admit defeat even when it happens every day? The fact is that Tordenskjold cheated the pants off the defenders by pretending that he had far more men than in reality. You see, he had guts and Swedes do not!'

A chorus of Norwegian voices shouted, 'hear, hear' and applause broke out.

At that moment, the guide had reached the large Norwegian but was diverted by Hans Erik's shouting. He grabbed Hans Erik's arm, but the Norwegian had predicted the move and moved forward, shirt-fronting the guide, who was a head shorter. The guide realised his mistake of overestimating his own capability, but he still held on to Hans Erik's arm. Hans Erik turned, attempting to free himself from the grip but ended up on the floor with the guide on top, and the Norwegian on his knees trying to break the guide's arm. The fight went on for a while, but eventually the guide reluctantly admitted defeat kicking his feet, with the Norwegian and Hans Erik sitting on top of him making it impossible to move. Four soldiers from the barracks had been called in and they split the fighting party, much to the dissatisfaction of the onlookers.

When the three men eventually stood up, the casualty became clear. The guide had a proper blue eye, his hat had flown over the rampart. His shirt and trousers were torn. Hans Erik shared a blue eye with the guide, but the Norwegian didn't have a scratch, only a sore jaw. In Nordic tradition, the soldiers forced the combatants to apologise to each other and to embrace. The embrace with the Swedish guide was only done reluctantly but was helped along when small glasses with Swedish "snaps" were distributed. They all sat down with the soldiers and shared the experience from the fighting, discussing tactical mistakes.

After a few more "snaps", the Norwegian, Hans Erik and

a proud Jacob, escaped from the fortress and deserted to the marina. The Norwegian was the captain of their neighbouring boat. The two men were not praised by their respective wives, but there was a bit of a cockpit party going on for a while, where old Nordic songs were sung. To the astonishment of the wives, people who walked along the dock stopped and complimented Hans Erik and the Norwegian on their achievement.

After a few glasses of wine, Hans Erik said to the Norwegian, hinting towards the endless stream of people complimenting them from the dock, 'Now I think I understand the idiom "Tordenskjold's soldiers".'

The following day, Grethe and Anne Mette took the bus on the mainland to Göteborg and caught the train towards Copenhagen, jumping off in Elsinore. Hans Erik and Jacob was escorted out of the archipelago by four Norwegian yachts which proudly flew their flags. Hans Erik was offered a nice piece of raw meat to cure his blue eye, but he declined. He was proud of his eye. The Norwegians waved goodbye as Hans Erik and Jacob sailed westward in a light, southerly breeze. Jacob steered and held the course while Hans Erik had an extended nap.

Seven hours later, Jacob went below to get his father off the bunk. He reported he had Hirsholmene straight ahead and awaited instructions. Hans Erik staggered on deck and looked out. 'I think the harbour is on the southern island. Go south and round the tip well off the coast before turning north.'

Hans Erik went below to have a wash and clear his head. Jacob had steered around the island. They started the motor, brought the sails down and Hans Erik steered Pitter into the harbour. They easily found a mooring and were welcomed by the harbour master.

Jacob and Hans-Erik decided to have a barbecue on shore. They had brought with them a small Turkish cast-iron barbecue, which they brought ashore with a bag of charcoal. Father and son were sitting in the sand with the hot barbecue on a rock.

They had finished all the meat and the accompanying bread and salad. Disregarding Hans Erik's sore, blue eye, that he carried with pride, they were happy.

An old man with a walking stick came from a cottage nearby towards Hans Erik and Jacob. His eyes were focused on the still glowing barbecue, not looking at anything else. He stared at the barbecue and with a small laugh, and in a strong dialect said, 'Look, look, it is coke!'

Hans Erik was puzzled, grabbed the bag of charcoal, showed it to the old man and said, 'No, it is charcoal,' and pointed at the bag.

The elderly man backed a few feet away, shook his head in wonder, and said with a surprised tone, 'Man knows little,' turned around and started to walk away. Hans Erik got up and asked, 'Sorry to stop you, but from where did you get the phrase, "man knows little"?'

The old man looked at Hans Erik with a fatherly smile and answered in his dialect, 'It's an old phrase. We have always used it here on the island. It is just a statement indicating that you have learned something new!'

The Island

It was late August and the autumn's storm season was held away by a comfortable high pressure. My wife and I decided to go sailing for a week. Our destination was the island of Anholt in the middle of the Skagerrak, some 55 NM North-west of Elsinore, or Helsingør as we Danes would call it. We left our departure too late, but we were used to sailing at night. It is a question of keeping a good lookout because, between the island of Sjælland and Anholt, there are many small fishing boats trawling for Norwegian lobster at night. There are also many ships coming from the north or south, but they usually followed a more easterly course, staying well away from all the treacherous sandbanks. Over time, many ships had been wrecked close to Anholt.

After battling winds from unexpected directions, we finally arrived in the harbour on the western side of the island. It was Sunday morning. We took our red dinghy to the jetty and walked to the shore, hoping to find a baker open, as is the tradition in Denmark.

It was a fresh walk from the harbour to the town for our weary sea legs. I was enjoying the landscape and all the birds, not taking much notice of anything else.

'Haven't you noticed,' my wife said, 'there are no people here?'

'Yes, you are right, there should be traffic to and from the harbour, and always people on bikes — now there are none.'

We walked a bit further, but still no sign of people.

'Honey,' I said, 'have you seen anybody?'

She did not answer.

As we walked on, I became uncomfortable. The island used to be a marvellous place for summer guests and yachties to enjoy, especially during the summer. In springtime, the eider ducks would be nesting among the flowering sea thrifts, and the terns would have a colony on the beach just outside the harbour. In late summer, there would still be retirees, but birdlife had slowed down.

'Remember,' I said to my wife, 'they used to have a beach market here, and all the kids were roasting marshmallows over a fire; now there is nothing.'

My wife did not answer. She just kept on walking in front of me. At every step, I got more worried. Why does she walk so fast, and why is she not talking? But she just walked. I could see the village among the windswept trees. It looked deserted. I suddenly felt a creeping feeling of sadness. I called my wife, but she did not turn around. She just walked.

When I reached the village road, my wife was far ahead of me. All the houses had stands of pink marshmallows along the walls. Suddenly, a man, dressed in black, came out of a door. He turned his back towards me and locked the door with a key. I thought islanders never locked their houses. He looked at me with a solemn face and walked down the road in a hurry. My wife was still ahead, just walking. I heard the church bells ringing briefly.

The bell ringing made me recall that Anholt has always been seen humorously as being backwards, ever since an eighteenth-century writer and poet wrote about a man called Peder Paars. He intended to visit his fiancée and sailed form Kalunborg with the intention of reaching Aarhus on Jutland. But he was shipwrecked on the beach by envious gods, just to be tempted by the daughter of the king's bailiff. He escaped her temptations and, therefore, kept his virtue intact.

Peder Paars and his crew meet the islanders and describe them as living as Christians but still plundered shipwrecks and castaways. The bailiff would always pass judgments to favour himself. Superstition was rife and despite the fact the island has accepted Protestantism — the priest still used the Catholic bible. It has even been suggested that, to this very day, there is a thriving satanic cult on the island.

My wife stopped in front of the church door. Sounds came from inside. After a while, the wide door swung open, and darkly dressed people came out. Women wore black veils; many had flowers in their arms. They walked to the cemetery. My wife joined the women. I sat down on a bench along a parapet wall in the shade of an old oak. An older man dressed in black carrying a walking stick came and sat next to me.

I asked, 'What is going on?'

He shook his head and said, 'Miss Marie Jensen used to come here every summer. We enjoyed her stories. Then she died, and a new lady author moved in. She wrote many stories, but they were all about anxiety, grief, and depression. Slowly, sadness crept into our lives, and it would not go away. Our doctor talked to the new author, but in vain. The doctor said that when she leaves in late summer, we will be better again. Our priest said that every Sunday we need to pray at Miss Jensen's grave and ask her to make the new lady author go away. That's what we do!'

The Single Hander

Grey sky with fleeing clouds,
birds glide over rustling shrouds.
Dark seas and rolling waves,
following the chorus of singing whales.

Grip files, grip files, checked and checked,
winds and water are flushing the deck.
Weather is coming but soon it's gone,
it is time to get up and face the dawn.

The vastness of an ocean makes everybody small,
loneliness is anybody's call.
Check the sails and check the sheaths,
ropes must be neat in every cleat.

Sitting in lee watching passing waves,
is to mislay what your bow will brave.
Thoughts are forged and dreams are born,
like welcome and embrace a newborn fawn.

The devil in the game is always there,
waiting for you to pay his fare.
His name is loneliness, and he is next to you,
ready to give your dreams a blow.

How to get rid of him, I do not know,
he is on my shoulder like a homeless crow.
But maybe he is there as Neptune's messenger,
calming the seas and a merciful educator.

I have put him away in a safe place below,
not to forget whether friend or foe.
He is here with me for good or bad,
if he left my boat, I would truly be sad.

This is the tale of a single hander,
who sails the seas as his own commander.
In his loneliness, he is never alone,
because loneliness' friendship is all he owns.

Shawline Publishing Group Pty Ltd
www.shawlinepublishing.com.au

More great Shawline titles can be found by scanning the QR code below.
New titles also available through Books@Home Pty Ltd.
Subscribe today at www.booksathome.com.au or scan the QR code below.